WALKING INTO HELLFIRE

In one brief instant Pete knew he was facing what he had feared most and what he had tried and sworn to avoid.

A gun was in Ben Mellish's hand and still Pete could not move, could not unlock his muscles. And then the gun went off. Pete felt the vicious blow to his shoulder and it threw him back and sideways against the door as the second shot blasted out, missing him.

He leapt to one side, swinging the gun up shoulder high. He shot five times, so quickly the third shot played counterpoint against Ben's third . . . .

Pete raised bleak eyes to Chris as she looked at him over the body of her dead brother—the brother he had killed. . . .

BRAND OF EMPIRE

Luke Short

A DELL BOOK

Published by
Dell Publishing
a division of
Bantam Doubleday Dell Publishing Group, Inc.
666 Fifth Avenue
New York, New York 10103

Published in serial form under the title "Red Trail to Black
Treasure"

The trademark Dell® is registered in the U.S. Patent and
Trademark Office.

ISBN: 0-440-10770-9

Reprinted by arrangement with The Estate of
Frederick D. Glidden

Printed in the United States of America

Published simultaneously in Canada

Four Previous Dell Editions

April 1989

10 9 8 7 6 5 4 3 2 1

KRI

CHAPTER ONE

OLD DOC BENBOW STIRRED and opened his eyes to darkness. For a moment, small panic stirred in him, and then he knew night had come and there was no light in his office. It took considerable effort to drag himself upright on the cracked-leather office sofa, but once erect he felt around his feet for the jug. It was there beside him, as it had been every awakening for twenty years. While he drank, the hushed clatter of Mrs. Carew's pots and pans in the kitchen came to him.

Feeling immediately better, he hauled himself to his feet and as he made his familiar way to the kitchen he snapped his galluses up over his wrinkled shirt.

Mrs. Carew, his indomitably neat and grim house-keeper, looked up from the stove as he entered.

"Morning," Doc said.

"Evenin'," Mrs. Carew replied, her voice at once correction and reproof, with perhaps a little affection.

At the sink in the corner of the tiny kitchen Doc ladled the basin full of water and took off his shirt. If there was anything humorous in his slack little paunch, his pipestem arms, his narrow freckled shoulders and pale skin, he was willing to share it with Mrs. Carew.

She said, "You need a shave."

Doc said without looking in the mirror, "So I do."

"There's hot water."

"So there is."

Doc went right ahead with his washing, making an inordinate amount of noise at it and deriving what seemed to Mrs. Carew an inordinate amount of pleasure out of splashing the kitchen.

He took down the towel and turned to confront her, a small man, erect of carriage, with a drink-flushed seamed face that had the sad jowl-droop of a springer spaniel. Looking at him, an observer would have thought that once, long ago, his eyes had been fine. In a way, they were still fine, if you could forget the whisky veins and concentrate on the humor, the skepticism, the kindliness in them. Blue, not dull even now, they told the true history of old Doc Benbow, a history of intelligence and idealism, of passionate labor, of skepticism, and lastly, of whisky-mellowed tolerance. His thick cap of dead silver hair was cut short, and every hair was standing on end now. There was also more than a suggestion of that silver-white stubble on his face.

Mrs. Carew said, "Go ahead. I'll wait supper."

"Wait for what?"

"Aren't you going to shave?"

"I am not," Doc said flatly. "This is my own home. I can run around naked here if I want."

"And drunk," Mrs. Carew said primly.

"And drunk," Doc echoed, without a trace of shame or sheepishness, as he put his shirt on. A sly look of deviltry appeared in his eyes. He said, "As a matter of fact, I think I'll do both. Will you join me?"

Mrs. Carew did not bother to answer, and Doc chuckled. She should have been used to his harmless ribaldry by now, but it seemed she wasn't. She took his supper from the warming-oven of the huge black stove and laid it out on the checkered cloth, then got her shawl and walked over to the back door. Doc sat down and surveyed the supper.

"Doctor Benbow," Mrs. Carew said quietly. Doc looked up. "I'm sorry about last night."

"What about last night?" Doc asked bluntly.

"About Frank Mellish."

Doc had a hot retort on his lips, but it died. He looked down at his hands, frowning at them, before he looked up at Mrs. Carew and with the old stubbornness in his voice said, "Sorry? I wouldn't say that. Even a hog has to die sometime."

"I didn't mean that. I meant about—about your losing him."

"All the king's horses and men couldn't put Humpty Dumpty together. And all the doctors this side of St. Louis couldn't have put Frank Mellish's head together." He smiled crookedly. "Funny, but I'd always thought he had such a thick skull it couldn't break."

"There'll be talk, though."

Doc said quickly, mildly, "Let them talk, damn them! Good night."

Mrs. Carew went out, but Doc didn't eat right away. He sat there staring at the table, his face musing, melancholy. He sighed then and muttered something and rose and went into his office. When he came back he was carrying his stone jug. He emptied his glass of milk in the sink and came back and filled it with whisky and drank off half of it.

Then he set about eating, feeling better, but Mrs. Carew had contrived to stir up something that whisky wouldn't dull. There would be talk, she had said. That was an understatement. There would be hell to pay. Frowning, Doc tried to recall what had happened since yesterday afternoon. At noon an Anchor rider on a blown pony had pulled up at the office, tramped in, and told Doc to come along, that Frank Mellish had a broken head. Doc was drunk then—there was no denying it—but no more drunk than usual. The Anchor puncher had almost foundered a livery team getting out to the Anchor by midnight.

The whole outfit was up at the big log house, ringed around Big Ben Mellish, who was standing over his brother Frank. Doc hadn't missed the open sneers of the hands when he'd hiccuped and staggered a little. Hell, a man couldn't ride in a cramped buckboard for twelve hours without being stiff. But when Doc saw Frank Mellish he hadn't been so fuddled that he couldn't tell Frank was going to die. A horse had pitched him, Ben said. Whatever had done it, Frank's head resembled the shell of a hard-boiled egg which has been dropped and rolled. The only thing holding it together was the scalp.

Doc had done all he could, but what was there to do? Frank Mellish just stopped breathing while Doc was gently determining the extent of the fracture.

Ben saw him die. He whirled on Doc, his deep voice strangled with fury. "You damned old sot, you've killed him!"

That had made Doc mad, unreasonably mad, and his retort was unwise as well as untrue. "What if I did! Did you expect me to cure him?" But even if he admitted doing so, Doc hadn't killed him.

Ben had struck him then, not hard, but contemptuously, as if he were cuffing a dog into obedience. It didn't matter that Doc fought back and was gently but firmly thrown in the buckboard. It did matter, however, that lawless Big Ben Mellish, standing there with the lantern while those tough, hard-fisted riders of his looked on, said, "Doc, you've served out your time here. You better clear out of Ten Troughs."

Someone had given the team a cut over the rumps with a rope end, and Doc didn't have time to answer before they bolted. He was two miles down the road before he had them under control, and then it didn't seem worth the trouble to return. A quart of whisky in his black bag helped to dull his anger on the way back, and sleep did the rest.

But now he was worried. He was too old to pick up and get out, too old to put up a fight, too fond of this groove to risk a change. He thought of his gun out there in the office and wondered if he could still use it.

A thundering knock at the door interrupted his reverie. He said loudly, "Come in," and waited. Nothing happened. Ben Mellish?

"Come in!" he shouted, and still nothing happened.

Swearing, Doc rose and picked up the lamp and walked over to the back door. Setting the lamp on the washstand, he yanked the door open. It swung back as if pushed, and something fell at Doc. Instinctively he dodged aside, but in the split second of doing it he saw this was a man toppling into the room, and Doc made a grab at him and missed. The figure fell heavily on its face on the floor.

For a moment Doc regarded him. The man's shirt had been cut to ribbons, and his broad back was wet with blood.

The jingle of a bridle and chain out in the dark shifted Doc's attention.

As if waiting for this, a hard voice cut through the night. "If he lives, Doc, tell him we'll be back for another."

Doc mumbled, "Wait," and reached for the lamp. He got it, stepped over the sill holding it over his head. The sharp, flat crack of gunshot hammered once, and the lamp blinked out in a tinkle of glass, which showered over Doc's head and wrist. Slowly he lowered the lamp, and listened to several horses pound out of the yard and down the back alley.

By the aid of matches Doc found another lamp over by the stove and lighted it and then observed the man on the floor, whose feet still prevented the door from closing. Leaning down, Doc turned him over and reached for his wrist, feeling for the pulse.

There was a flutter there. Obviously the man was a cowhand, for he wore the saddle-soft Levi's and boots of a cattlehand; but there was no familiar clue in his looks— nor would there ever be, Doc thought grimly. If the man had been his own son, Doc could not have recognized him. Under the matted black hair the face was not a face. It had been beaten and kicked until the eyes were closed, the nose mashed, the mouth a shapeless scar. The chest and shoulders, bare under the torn shirt, were livid with bruises and cuts.

He's been flogged, Doc thought, straightening up, remembering the raw flesh of his back. *Beat up, kicked, flogged.*

Doc looked at him curiously. Some sudden pride in him made him want to save this parcel of clubbed and beaten flesh, just as a protest against Big Ben Mellish and his kind and all that they believed and said.

While the water was boiling, Doc staggered into the bedroom with the man and dumped him on the clean bed in this spartan room; and then Doc prepared for the night. He should have had someone come in to help, but his pride precluded that, too.

He worked like a slave—and he drank, too, more as a gesture than from need, but occasionally he was glad of the whisky, for the job was not pleasant.

When the first smoke of the breakfast fires was lifting over Ten Troughs, Mrs. Carew arrived at Doc's. She found the kitchen in a litter of slopped water, blood, and bandages; and pervading everything was the smell of disinfectant. She was well enough versed in the life of a doctor that it did not surprise her. Stepping gingerly, she opened the door to Doc's room.

There, in the bed, was a bandage-swathed figure, face to the ceiling, two slits left for the eyes and nose, another for the mouth. Mrs. Carew couldn't tell if the thing in bed was a man or woman until she caught sight of the bloody clothes.

And in the lone easy chair in all this house, Carlyle's *Sartor Resartus* open on his chest, head slumped back, mouth open, face weary and still unshaven, old Doc Benbow slept. Behind him, the lamp was still burning. Beside him, the jug was corked neatly.

This was Mrs. Carew's introduction to Pete Yard, once removed from a corpse.

CHAPTER TWO

BEFORE DAWN, Christina Mellish slipped out of bed and dressed hurriedly against the cold of the early spring morning. Leaving her room, she descended to the first floor and paused in the door of the big living-room. From this same door she had watched Doctor Benbow last night. Somehow, she thought, that scene epitomized the Mellishes, with its violence, its tragedy, and its ruin. Frank dying on the table, a crew of reckless, silent men around him, while Ben, who should have protected Frank in the first place, who should have bowed to dignity on this occasion, turned it into a brawl with his bullying. She felt only disgust instead of grief.

In the far corner, a clutter of gear strewn on the floor around him, Frank was stretched out on the cot under a gray blanket, still in his riding-clothes. Slowly Chris took the two steps down into the room and walked toward him. Paused beside him, she was about to lift the blanket when a slight movement on the couch behind her arrested her. The gesture died and she straightened and turned to see Ben, restless in a light sleep, on the couch.

A momentary pity stirred within her, softening the stilled warmth of her face, so that the bright-green dress she had chosen this morning out of a deep and hard defiance, seemed brash and gay. But it was only for a moment, and then her face was composed, cold, and modeled slimly, with more arrogance in the full lips than she knew. The early light touched her hair, turning its straight tawniness to an ash-gray. Ben grunted a little and thrashed over, trying to bury his face in the hard leather of the couch. Again Chris regarded Frank, but the moment of privacy and small grief was gone, and she turned away toward the kitchen wing of the house, her walk proud and free.

Two hours later she was standing on the long porch that tied both single-story wings to the main house. She had almost forgotten that the triangle out in the cookshack had clanged minutes ago, and that Ben would be up soon. The sun was just beginning to touch the broad basin below her when he tramped out onto the porch where the breakfast table was set for two. He looked sharply at her and said, "Hallo, Chris."

"Hallo, Ben."

Christina did not immediately sit down. She allowed Sarah, the Ute cook, to bring out Ben's breakfast while she stood watching the shadows in the Basin below dissolve first into purple-misted flats and tilting plains, then gradually, like a miniature continent moving up out of the sea, rise into the rolling grama-grass benches which was the Anchor range. Immediately below her, the foothills dwindled into piñon-stippled swells before they blended into the ocean of grass that was broken by the rugged mesas beyond, and beyond them, the clean, lofty lines of the rock-gaunted Ute peaks already bright in the hot sun. And then day was here, clean, clear, proud, and she turned to observe Ben.

He was bent over his breakfast, a giant of a man with square, overwide shoulders that made everything he touched toylike. He had changed his soiled clothes of yesterday for clean waist overalls and dark shirt and vest.

"You've eaten?" he asked, his voice deep and rumbling and warm—spuriously so, Chris thought. She sat down opposite him, and Sarah brought her breakfast. Ben studied her covertly, disapproving of the gay color of her dress, a little awed by the clear, still beauty of her face, that this morning was so still and contained. Long since he had learned that the gray wide eyes mirrored her temper, but they were not friendly today! They were as cold and hard and unmoved as agate, not pretty, too hard for a slight girl who believed herself a woman.

"The world still seems to go around," Ben said quietly, a calculated note of sadness in his voice.

"Stop that, Ben!" Chris said. Ben looked up and found her eyes changed. They were angry now, and the clean line of her jaw was defiant. It irritated Ben Mellish, as most things did nowadays, so that his crafty, long face held momentary petulance. The son of the man who had built this cattle domain with courage and shrewdness, Ben was heir to a great legacy, but legacies have a way of thinning out; and Dave Mellish, while he had deeded a fortune to his son, had not deeded with it the power to hold it nor the looks to bluff. Ben's dark, weather-burned face flushed a little and he said, "You aren't sorry, then?"

"I mourned Frank a year ago, Ben," Chris said calmly. She nodded to his breakfast. "Eat it. There will be time to talk afterward."

"Talk about what?"

"You shall see."

They finished breakfast in silence, and Ben shoved his plate away and tilted his chair back, rolling a cigarette. Observed now, he was an almost handsome man, assuredly a strong one, but there was a stubbornness, a petty ruthlessness in the square set of his small head on his overwide shoulders that argued a lack of both mercy and pity. And those two things, Christina was thinking, were what she most needed today.

Sarah cleared the dishes away and only then did Ben speak.

"Get it over," he said bluntly. "What did you mean by saying you mourned Frank a year ago?" He smiled meagerly now, showing his even strong teeth a little wolfishly. "Or am I supposed to want to quarrel with my sister on the day our brother is to be buried?"

Chris looked up at him quickly, her face coloring. "It won't be a quarrel, Ben. I'm almost afraid to. Or does your chivalry which doesn't include a helpless old man make an exception of a woman?"

Ben flushed now. His chair came to the floor and he leaned over the table, his voice tight with anger. "Now that's enough!"

"More than enough."

Ben looked at her hotly. "You saw it, then?"

"From the corridor."

"Did you see what the drunken old fool did?" he asked harshly. "Did you see—"

"He touched him, Ben. Just as you touched him when you brought him in."

"He killed him!"

"He did not!"

Ben glared at her, and Chris met his stare unswervingly. Ben started to rise out of his chair and then he sat down again.

"I'd leave, Chris, but I want to hear the rest of this. You didn't want to talk about this alone."

Chris shook her head. Her slim hands were folded on the table, and it was she who leaned a little forward now, her face serious, determined, but her voice was without anger as she asked, "Ben, where did Frank get hurt?"

"I told you. He was riding that half-broken dun gelding. Down there on Cinquo Forks where the trail slopes steep to the canyon bottom, something spooked his horse. It shied off the trail and Frank was thrown. He rolled to the bottom of the gorge. When the boys got there he was just the way you saw him."

"That's a lie," Chris said quietly.

Ben came to his feet, his chair crashing over behind him. Towering over her, both hands on the table, he said thickly, "I won't take that from anybody, Chris—not even my sister!"

"Yes, you will," Chris said, still quietly. "You'll take it from me now, Ben—but it will be the last time you'll have to. I say you lie." She smiled contemptuously. "I've listened to so many lies from you and Frank this last year that I'm a connoisseur of them. Would you like to know how I know you lie?"

Without waiting for his answer, she said, "Frank left here day before yesterday saying he was riding over to the reservation to see the agent about a hay deal. The reservation is south. Lin Kennedy met him and three of our hands twenty-five miles up the Basin near Lett's Ferry. I know that because Kennedy volunteered the information when I was over there yesterday."

"Then the men who brought him back lied to me," Ben said sullenly.

"They did not. You knew where he had been, Ben. You know because Charlie Schrader has a bullet hole in his arm. Sarah told me that. And Charlie was with Frank."

The color started to mount in Ben's neck, and Chris watched him without emotion. She knew he was slow-witted, and she gave him time to frame his answer. Ponderously, he sat down and lit his cigarette, which had gone out.

"All right," he said suddenly, "he was up near Lett's

Ferry. What about it?"

"What's your story now? How did he get killed?"

"He was drunk." Ben blurted out. "He fell off his horse going down into the canyon. He really did."

"And Charlie's arm?"

"That was more of their horseplay. I—I didn't want you to know he was drinking."

"And that's another lie," Chris said evenly. "Frank wasn't a coward, but there was one thing he wouldn't do, and that is ride a horse when he'd been drinking. Maybe you don't remember the time he was dragged in here, one foot in the stirrup, after he'd been drinking in town and had gone to sleep in the saddle?"

Ben held his sullen silence, his eyes murky and angry.

"It won't do, Ben," Chris continued. "You see, I know how Frank was killed."

"How?"

"He was beaten up. He had it coming to him."

Instead of being angry, now Ben said nothing. He smoked in silence, watching Chris, but the deep inhalation he took from his cigarette betrayed his excitement, and his eyes avoided hers.

"And who beat him up?" he drawled presently.

"I don't know. You do. I dare say they're dead now."

Ben dropped his cigarette when she said it, and he did not attempt to pick it up. Sitting ramrod-straight in the chair, his big hands fisted at his sides, he stared at her. "So I'm a murderer now?"

"I can't tell yet," Chris said evenly, "but I think you are. You've murdered in the past."

Ben contrived to laugh deeply, although it was not hearty. He started to rise, when Chris's voice cut out sharp and strong. "Sit down, Ben! You'll only have to listen to this once!"

Ben sat still, waiting, as if wanting to humor her, but the skin around his lips was pale, and his dark eyes smoldered.

"For a year now I've been lied to by you and Frank. I was supposed to be blind, as well as stupid. Do you think these poor ranch women up in the north end of the Basin haven't talked to me? Do you think their children haven't shied rocks at me? Do you think I haven't heard about them moving—moving out because the women are afraid of what will happen to their children? Do you think I can't tell the difference between a loyal cowhand and the brand of gunmen you've been hiring? Do you think I don't notice it when I go into a store and people fall silent? Do you think I haven't noticed these men who ride up here at night to talk in your office and who are gone by morning? Do you?"

Ben rumbled tolerantly, "Go on."

"There was a time when an Anchor rider was a sort of ambassador, Ben. People listened to him, respected him, because he was just about the ablest cowboy that ever sat a horse. He had to be, or our father wouldn't hire him. Do you remember the time when a band of Utes rode up here from the reservation to return three Anchor steers, Ben? Every one else on this range was shooting at Utes, on principle, because of their thievery. Do you remember?"

Ben said nothing. Chris rose. "I think I'll leave before everybody on this range starts shooting at Anchor riders on principle."

Ben said darkly, "Frank's being buried this morning."

Chris looked at him a long time, studying his face, trying to look beyond the smoky anger in his eyes.

"You won't tell, then?" she asked.

"There's nothing to tell," Ben drawled in his deep cavernous voice.

"Then I'm going."

Ben said, "How will you live?"

"I don't know. Other women do."

"You won't get a cent from me," Ben said quietly, stubbornly. "When you ride off this place, it's to stay. If you ever come back, I'll have you thrown off!"

"I believe that."

"You'd better," Ben said grimly, rising. "I said Frank is going to be buried this morning. Will you wait?"

Chris had her back turned to him now, and she was glad that he could not see her face. She hesitated a moment before she spoke, and then answered in a dead voice, "I buried Frank a year ago, Ben—the only Frank that was a man. No. I won't stay."

"Suit yourself."

"I'll want a buckboard and a man to drive me to town. Will you give it to me?"

"The sooner the better."

Mounting the stairs again, Chris's eyes were dry, her back straight, but somehow her legs were leaden and the despair she felt seemed part of her blood and breath.

In her room, packing, she suddenly discovered that she was crying, but she would not recognize it. Moving with a kind of mechanical precision, she managed to get most of her belongings in one trunk; and all the time her face was wet with tears. Not for Frank, for she had meant what she said; and not for Ben, who, to her, was irrevocably lost; but because she was leaving this place of fine tradition, of her childhood, and of every cherished memory she had. Somehow her defiance was not quite so undiluted as she neared the end of her packing, and when the trunk lid was shut she sat on it and wept bitterly.

Later, when her trunk had been taken out and she was ready to go, she walked down into the big room. Its floor and walls were bright with Indian blankets; its rawhide chairs were deep and worn, smelling of riding-gear and leather, its fireplace massive and blackened. All of her life had centered here, but she strode through the room without looking at it, afraid to pause.

Ben stood on the porch, and beyond him the buckboard and team were waiting, the driver patient. Her sorrel gelding was tied to the endgate of the buckboard and she could see her saddle beside the trunk.

"I've been thinking," Ben said curtly. "This place is partly yours. But you needn't plan to claim your share."

"I won't."

Ben looked down at her, puzzled. He was wearing a gun, ready to ride. Chris knew he had made a concession in waiting to bid her good-by. The only times he looked at her were when she was not looking at him, and she felt his eyes probing, sardonic, surly, through his effort to seem casual.

"Why not?" he asked.

This time Chris caught his eyes and held them, and her voice was passionless as she said, "Because you'll be killed, Ben. I'll let the ranch stay whole." And she went down the steps.

The driver, a cowhand, helped her in, and Chris did not look at Ben as they drove off. Later, on the road below, she turned to look at the spread. It sprawled there in all its massive log dignity in that small bench among the lodgepoles. Behind it were the log barns and sheds and corrals, all touched by the calico pattern of the sun through the near pines.

She said to the cowhand, "Stop, Ed."

The team pulled up, and Chris got out. She lifted her saddle and bridle from the buckboard, saying, "I'll ride in. You leave the trunk at the hotel," and untied her sorrel's lead rope.

So this was the way she said good-by to the Anchor, by riding over its range, and she felt better for it as she crossed the line fence and headed string-straight for Ten Troughs in midafternoon.

CHAPTER THREE

WITHIN TWO DAYS Christina had exhausted the possibilities for work in Ten Troughs. People were kind, exceedingly kind, and, when she had received their sympathy over Frank's death and the amenities had been satisfied, they listened. They did not ask questions, for her very manner showed they would be unwelcome. But gradually, behind the veil of their friendliness and consideration, she began to perceive what she was up against. She was invited to stay with friends, to keep her room at the Exchange rent-free until her affairs were straightened out, but as for work, there was none. People laughed, or if they were more polite they smiled. Ten Troughs already had a schoolteacher. What else was there for a woman to do?

Manfred Pearson, the owner of the Pearson Emporium, asked her this.

"But, Mr. Pearson," she pleaded, as that kind old friend of her father's listened patiently, "for ten years you've been moaning that it drove you crazy to keep books. So you don't. You make money, but only the Lord knows how."

"I don't, and that's a fact." Pearson smiled.

"All right, I've kept the Anchor books since father died. I've kept them well, too. I can keep yours."

"But you're a woman."

"But I can keep books!"

Pearson shook his head, not understanding. "A woman keeping books for an old Indian trader? It won't do. It's such a rotten job I won't even do it myself."

"But I will."

Again Pearson shook his head. "Keeping a count of cows is different from counting bolts of calico, dozens of buttons, cartridges, and flour. No. I won't let you work. If you need money I'll give it to you. If you need a home, ours is open, and you're welcome. But as for putting you to work, why—why, I'd be ashamed to."

There was no place for her, it seemed. She could live genteelly on charity and her friends, but she could not pay her way. The stupidity of it galled her, and more than that, it frightened her.

She glanced at the clock as she left Pearson. Outside, she paused on the steps of the Emporium and looked over the somnolent main street of this town, wondering if she had overlooked a single chance. Thinking this, her eyes settled on the Melodian saloon across the dusty street. A score of hipshot ponies stood in the sun-bathed street at its hitchrack, and from its dark depths the jangle of a piano reflected a tinny gaiety. Occasionally she could hear one of the dance-hall girl's loud laughter. It seemed there was one way a woman could make her living here, she thought bitterly, and stepped off onto the boardwalk, heading for the hotel and another meal, and another afternoon of furious impotence.

She heard a voice behind her say gruffly, "When I first laid eyes on you, your legs weren't nearly that long."

Chris smiled, even before she turned, for this could be only Doctor Benbow, the single man of her acquaintance who would dare to refer to her legs. She waited for him to catch up with her and take her arm. His black hat rode his head at a jaunty angle, and today he was clean-shaven, the smell of bay rum mingling not unpleasantly with the sweet odor of whisky on his breath.

They walked a way in silence, and then Doctor Benbow said, "What's this I hear about your living in town?"

"It's true. But I don't know for how long." She paused. "You see, I need work, and I can't get it."

"Why should you?" Doc muttered. "Leave the jobs for those that need them."

"But I need it!" Chris said, turning her face to him, and he saw her gray eyes were troubled. "I—I've left, Uncle Doc—left the Anchor for good."

Doc stopped and pulled her around to face him. Casually he looked at her from head to foot, approving of the gray gabardine suit with its full skirt and wide-sleeved short jacket. Her small black hat was redeemed from severity by the rich sleekness of her hair, touched now by the sun.

"Left for good," he echoed, and she nodded, flushing a little.

"Good," Doc said gruffly. "High time."

Chris patted his hand and held it, and said softly, "You see, there is one Mellish who can remember the old Anchor and who—who—"

"Doesn't like its ways now."

"Yes."

Two cowpunchers in their high-heeled boots approached, listening to the grave talk of a Ute between them. When the three of them saw Doctor Benbow and

Christina their conversation ceased. One of the punchers said, "Mornin', Miss Mellish, Doc," and touched his hat, but the other, hand almost raised to his hat, looked away. Chris recognized him as one of the ranchers up in the north end of the Basin, and the man's action did not escape Doc. When they were past, Chris said, "I think that tells it all, doesn't it?"

Doc was silent a moment, and then he said without looking at Chris, "What happened out there the other night—it wasn't that, was it?"

"Just one of the things."

"I'm sorry about that—about the fighting, I mean," Doc muttered. "I was drunk, I reckon."

"Not drunk on anger and power and greed, Uncle Doc, like Ben was."

"No," Doc said, and presently added, "No."

At the hotel steps they paused, and Doc said without any preliminary, "Look here, Chris, I'm in a hole."

Chris waited, and Doc said bitterly, "I reckon gratitude is dead—dead and buried and forgotten in these times. I never thought she'd do it."

"Who, Uncle Doc?"

"Mrs. Carew, that—that good woman," and Doc contrived to get more contempt in those two words than if he had cursed.

"But why?"

Doc took a deep breath and growled, "For twenty years, I've kept her, given her work—and easy work—and now the first time I really need her, she balks, deserts me."

This was a lie, Chris knew, because Doc was fonder of his housekeeper than anyone else, and the feeling, in spite of Mrs. Carew's primness, was mutual. Chris smiled secretly and took her cue.

"The wretch," she murmured in mockery. "What has she done now?"

"She won't nurse."

"I don't blame her. She's your housekeeper."

"Well and good, but it's the duty of a housekeeper to keep what's in the house, isn't it?"

Chris smiled. "Technically, I suppose."

"All right, I have a patient in the house. He needs constant care. Mrs. Carew has refused to do it." He looked at her, his blue eyes questioning. "Not only that, but all the women in this town—the good women—suddenly find they are busy. They've got to watch kids or are watching the kids that are about to come." He sniffed. "More of Mrs. Carew's work. She's set them against me. Now I don't know who to turn to." He said gravely, less violently, "Who would you recommend?"

Chris felt her throat ball up. In his kind, private way Doctor Benbow was offering her work, and he tried to put it as tactfully as he knew how. She was grateful to him, and she knew he would deny he was trying to do her a favor. She guessed that poor Mrs. Carew, who kept the doctor's household as well as her own, was overburdened with work, and that she would be grateful for help. At least this would not be charity. So Chris smiled and said, "Do you want me to recommend a wonderful woman, an expert nurse?"

"If you can. I doubt it."

"I can."

"Who?"

"Myself."

Doc scowled and pursed his lips and finally shook his head. "That won't do—not after what Ben said."

"What Ben said was bluster," Chris told him. "Are you afraid he'll come and hurt me, Uncle Doc?"

"Nonsense. It'll be me, and if he tries it at all he'll do it in public. But it's you I'm thinking of. He won't like it."

Chris laid a hand on his arm and said, "I'm hired, then? I'll be over this evening." She put the time late so that Doc might have time to warn Mrs. Carew of his defamation of her character.

Doc sighed and said, "All right. But just temporarily to help me out—until I can get a woman who knows something." His rare smile took the barbs from this shaft and he walked away. At the Melodian, a few minutes later, Doc approached the bar and watched the bartender bring down his bottle. Forgetfully, Doc leaned up against the bar and backed away again with a grimace. The skin on his stomach was pinched where it had caught between the bar and the worn Colt he had rammed in his belt underneath the vest. He was carrying one now.

Doc took his noon drinks alone, and he was enough of a fixture here that the percentage girls ignored him and only the men who had business to do joined him. He was thinking that Ben Mellish would not like this, that Mrs. Carew would protest it as an unnecessary expenditure, and that the patient very likely did not have the money to pay for it. *Damn them all,* he thought stubbornly, and set about enjoying his drink.

Doctor Benbow's office was just off the main four corners of Ten Troughs, across the alley from the side and rear of the Pearson Emporium. The building itself was a single-story scabrous affair of peeled paint with the usual false front to make it appear doubly tall. It faced the street, but the door had been sealed into a window, so that the only entrance was from the alley. On the corner of the building was a sign which once read: *Horace L. Benbow, M.D.,* but that was fifteen years ago, the day of its painting. It had signified that, even though he was then middle-aged, this was Doctor Benbow's first private practice. It was hung up just exactly one month after Doc had been cashiered from the Army Medical Corps for drinking.

Now it was merely a board with a few flakes of sun-blistered black paint where the letters used to be. In its lower right-hand corner, where for some reason the oil of its white paint had been more tenacious, a clenched hand with finger pointing to the alley was still visible. Day and night, winter and summer, the finger pointed toward the cinder alley with such persistence that newcomers to Ten Troughs had been known to walk down the alley with furtive curiosity. The flowering geranium behind the clean curtains in the front window was also misleading, and of interest only to Mrs. Carew. Doc ignored it mostly, and swore at it occasionally, for it was beside his roll-top desk and he hated the smell of it.

To the side of Doc's office was the consulting-room, which was dusty and full of medical journals and empty bottles and books and miscellaneous trash. Doc had not once used it since he put it in under the impression that patients desire privacy. Perhaps they did; he never asked them. The cracked-leather sofa opposite the glass-front cabinet of instruments was at once the waiting-room, the operating-table, the dentist chair, and the most comfortable seat in the house; and the inflow of patients was such that none of its duties conflicted with the others. Best of all, Doc liked to read on it, putting the lamp on the rickety table at one end of the sofa.

He was about to do so this night, when Chris's knock sounded on his door and she entered. Doc took her wraps and then showed her to the kitchen, where she and Mrs. Carew visited a moment while Doc lighted a lamp and went into the bedroom.

He looked down at the man in the bed and, as always, he felt his curiosity awaken. Traditionally a doctor is supposed to take no interest in his patients other than a professional one and sometimes he has a difficult time doing that, but this was an exception. Doc wondered. Times were troubled now in this Basin, and a man might expect anything, but Doc had heard no mention of an open quarrel, nor of a rider missing.

He heard the sharp intake of breath behind him and he turned to observe Chris looking down at the man in the bed.

"Who is he?" Chris asked, her gray eyes troubled.

Doc shrugged.

"But—is he alive? What happened to him?"

"A beating," Doc said laconically. "A beating and a kicking and a flogging—especially a flogging."

"Will he live?"

"If he eats and sleeps enough. He's like a baby with a full-grown body. Most of his functions have been arrested by the shock. He can only take certain thin foods—soups and such. I don't even know if he can talk. Certainly, he hasn't yet. When he's awake he simply watches me with that one good eye." Doc smiled a little at this last. "Good eye, did I say? It's bad. Or if not bad, then hard, and assuredly unforgiving." He looked at her. "Well? Do you want the job?"

"Of course," Chris said softly, but something inside her shrank from the thought of this. She looked gravely at Doctor Benbow. "Beaten. By whom?"

Doc told her briefly all that he knew, how the man had been left, and the promise made by that night rider out in the dark. Chris watched Doc's eyes as he told it, and when he finished she asked quickly, "You didn't recognize the voice?"

"No." And he added, "It isn't that," quietly, knowing what she was thinking.

Chris looked down at the man again. "That isn't cattle-land's way," she murmured slowly. "They kill, yes, but not—not this."

"Unless the man is too big to kill. Or if they want to make an example of him."

"Example?"

Doc nodded slowly. "Whoever is responsible for it," he said thoughtfully, "is probably around my age. He isn't young, for that's not a young man's way of punishing. Also, he must have read history, else how would he know that severe flogging does more than hurt a man, that it breaks him, destroys him?" He meditated a moment, his glance returning to the figure. "In other days it was a punishment reserved for slaves and for the lowborn. And that," Doc added gently, "is where the flogger made his mistake."

"Then his spirit isn't broken, you mean."

"Watch his eyes," Doc said briefly. "If the flogger wanted to be safe, he should have killed him." Then Doc talked of other things, pointing out the medicines which Chris was to give, naming the feeding-times, the care.

Afterward he went back into his office. On his desk was the collected and unopened mail for something like a week. Since nothing ever arrived in the mail that was important to him, Doc only glanced at it when he had nothing better to do. His letters he only shuffled, opened a few at random and dumped the rest in the wastebasket. The two newspapers, one the weekly *State Register* from Toolle to the south, he leafed through, and then rose and took them in to Chris. Returning, he set the jug beside him and chose a book to read. It was *Henry IV*, which, like Carlyle, could best be enjoyed when a man was a little drunk.

In the bedroom Chris settled down to her task, which was merely waiting. The calm of this room, combined with the thoughts she could not prevent running through her mind, made her uneasy and sad. This now was only a stopgap, the prelude to the unknown, where security was only a word and a distant goal, not reality.

She picked up the *Register* and unfolded it and immediately her eye fell on a double-column headline: *Government to Build Dam at Antelope Butte*. For a moment she stared at it, and then it occurred to her that it referred to their Antelope Butte, the one at the head of the Basin. Here, interested, she read on, but the report was meager and indefinite, saying nothing beyond what the headlines told. The details would be published later in full, with specifications, dates of bidding on contracts, and such. The main purpose of the dam and reservoir was to impound water for the use of the Utes, on the reservation to the south below Ten Troughs, whom the government was endeavoring to aid in the transition from a hunting people to a farming people, the article said. The account ran over to the back page, and the last sentence of it said, *Authorities in Washington hinted that the announcement was premature, but that this was necessary so as to put rumors of speculation at rest.*

Chris read it again and then took the paper and went through the empty kitchen to Doc's office. He was stretched out on the sofa, his shoes beside the jug on the floor. He did not rise, merely looked over his book.

"Did you see this about the new dam?" Chris asked.

"I did."

"Is it good news?"

Doc only stared at her for a minute, then cleared his throat. "For hoemen, yes."

"But not for us ranchers?"

"Certainly. But the irrigable land will rise in value until it's too expensive to ranch on. Then we'll have fences, then fights, then farmers."

Chris laughed a little. "That's concise, anyway."

"It also happens to be true," Doc said.

"But why wasn't I told?" Chris demanded. "I've been in town two days now and no one has mentioned it."

Doc looked at his fingernails with a ferocious frown. "You're a woman," he said.

"But what of it?"

"The only sort of dams women are supposed to be interested in are the kind you tie around babies," Doc growled. "Now go away and let me read."

In the bedroom Chris wondered. Surely everyone in town knew it but they had not told her. And why had Doc faltered when she asked why she hadn't been told?

Sitting down beside the lamp she read the article again, and halfway through it the meaning suddenly came to her, and for a moment she was breathless. Of course! This was what Ben and Frank were preparing for. They had known about the dam. It explained these savage secret quarrels between the Anchor and the ranchers at the north end of the Basin, accounted for the rumor that the Mellish boys were determined to drive away ranchers who could not be bought off. It also accounted for those riders who came at night to confer with Ben and Frank and who were gone before morning. It explained—

"May I see that?" a voice asked suddenly, and Chris jumped with fright. It was the man in the bed. Slowly she rose and went over to him. His eyes were open now, and the one that was not bruised was a sort of gold hazel color, opaque, staring.

"What—what did you say?" Chris asked, and then before he could answer she made her own question nonsensical by adding, "I don't think you should."

He stirred a little as if in protest and said from between

the bandages, "The paper."

Chris stooped and picked it up, wondering how long she had been watched. She offered it to him, but he did not move his arms, which were under the sheet. "Hold it up, miss."

She obeyed. She watched the eye traverse the lines of print until her arm was tired. Then he said, "Back page, miss, please."

She turned it over. He could be reading only the article she had just read. She watched him come to the end, saw his eye hold the last line, and then he turned his head away. The bandage around his mouth shifted a little, as if he might be smiling.

"I'm supposed to feed you now," she said quietly.

The head turned and now the eye looked at her. It was disconcerting, for the gaze was alert, staring, with a quality of brashness in it that Chris could not analyze.

The man cleared his throat. He said, "Miss, when they brought me in here, did I have a gun?"

Without knowing why, Chris shook her head.

"You reckon you could get me one?" the voice drawled, and the head turned toward the wall. "I'll be needing it, I believe. I know."

CHAPTER FOUR

THE RICH POCKET of the Ten Troughs Basin lay just below the junction of the Raft River Range with the Utes, so that its world was bound by these mountains and reached out to the south, to the reservation, and beyond that to the plains and the desert. Of the eastern slope of the Raft River Range, Ten Troughs had heard little and cared less, perhaps because it was their tradition to look westward as the medicine for discontent, and there was no need of this medicine. Or perhaps it was because this Raft River Range walled out the east, shouldering skyward in rugged and forbidding peaks that held snow a good part of the year.

But if they knew little of the other side of this range, they had heard its legends, and the Great Western Cattle Company was one of them. They never saw its riders, and few had seen its range, but the boundaries of this barony had been staked out and won while their fathers were still fighting Utes from within the tight circle of a wagon train. They knew its range, a great apron of grass and timber that flanked the eastern slope and wheeled south to meet the Ute reservation and then traveled endless days over the eastern prairie of the Raft River Bench until it sloped into the badlands of Walking River.

A President had claimed shelter at its main house; a Grand Duke had hunted antelope on its plains, but that was in the past, when Matthew Waranrode, its owner, was young and preferred buckskin to broadcloth and was fighting unsuccessfully for a railroad spur up from the new transcontinental line. It was only when Matthew Waranrode became senator that people heard about the grand duke, and then it didn't matter so much. Didn't Matt Waranrode head every charity, and had his office in the state capital ever refused a worthy man a loan? Didn't the state get more than its share of the Federal bounty while he fought for the interest of the ranchers against the coming of the farmers? Was there a single huge ranch in this state (except his own) that could buy and bribe and terrorize? Was there any large-scale rustling? Hadn't his gargantuan barbecues endeared him to every voter in the state, and was he too proud to mingle with his people?

He was not, for Matthew Waranrode had read of bread and circuses. A month of them, for which he let his trim silver mustache grow ragged and for which he dressed in a baggy frock coat, put on cowman's boots, and smoked a pipe which he disliked, was a small enough price to pay for months of isolation and privacy at the G.W., of protection against this rabble he served.

But while Senator Waranrode gave only lip service to the open-handed tradition of this country, he did not despise the country itself. When he had first set eyes on it, a stalwart, domineering young rider in Tennessee homespun, he had loved it, loved especially this small emerald valley nestling in the folds of the Raft River foothills, and it was there he resolved to build. It had taken him ten years to get the money from his freighting-concessions to the new army posts to the south, but once he had it he returned, and this time with a crew of Mexican laborers. Always ambitious, he built big, and out of the native stone; and the style was that of the south and unfamiliar to the laborers. As his fortunes increased, wings were added; but when the reservations and forts supplied a ready market for his beef, these same wings were torn down, leaving only the original building with its wide gallery across the front. The quarters of men, the sheds, and the corrals were moved away from the house, so that it stood alone, under the huge cottonwoods and oaks, flanked by shrubs and orchards, a monument to a prosperity which could afford aloofness.

A hundred yards away, and down near the creek, the stone bunkhouse squatted with its back to the house. There the Mexican laborers had left their imprint, for the bunkhouse and cookshack, the wagon sheds, barns, blacksmith shop, and corrals formed a rough plaza, hiding the long sweep of valley to the south. This was the ranch, the heart of the G.W., as plain and practical and informal as a thousand of its kind, for Matthew Waranrode was first a cattleman, and second a self-made aristocrat.

On this night Senator Waranrode excused himself immediately after dinner and went upstairs to his study. One of his contradictions was that he liked to drink champagne in range clothes, and he had done so tonight, more to impress his guest than from pleasure, however. A man closer to the range than this lawyer-congressman downstairs would have noted that the senator's boots were more walked in than ridden in, his short coat more tailored than worn, his white shirt more starched than easy; but this congressman, in all truth, had been more attentive to Sylvia Waranrode than to her father.

The senator did not speak to the man waiting for him in his study, but immediately crossed to his desk in the corner. And Ames Manderfield, the man waiting for him, did not seem to expect it. Indeed, there seemed to be a familiarity between this straight, spare man and his less straight, sparer foreman that went deeper than friendship and touched need.

Ames Manderfield was the kind of man who would never be taken for anything other than a Texan, which he was not. Sandy straight hair, a little awry on a narrow head, bleach eyes that held neither depth nor color, and a thin, wide mouth that gave at the corners into lean cheeks and lent him an air of quiet command. The rest of him was cowman, from the scuffed high boots to the soiled neckerchief. He was from Mississippi by way of Texas and the Nations, and he was tough to the very unplumbed core of him.

The senator swung his chair so that his back was to the lamp on the sleek desk top, and reached for the pile of mail Ames had brought in. From it he first drew out a newspaper and slapped it open and read it, dark eyes a little mocking, less inscrutable than usual under the heavy white brows. Turning the paper over, he finished reading, and the ends of his trim white mustache curved up a little with a smile. He quoted in a mocking voice, "'Authorities in Washington hinted that the announcement was premature, but that this was necessary so as to put rumors of speculation at rest.'" He laid the paper down. "That's mild, anyway."

"Do you reckon Trueblood wrote it, though?" Ames drawled.

"Why not? He's written worse about me these five years past."

"It's too tame. It don't name names, and that's what he likes."

The senator chuckled. "He's afraid of libel. There are some things you can't print without proof, not even in that tin-pot, backbrush newspaper of his." He leafed through the rest of his mail, first lighting a cigar. Finding the letter he wanted, he opened and read it and then passed it on to Ames, who read it while Waranrode observed, "He was too late to stop that. How do you like the name?"

"'Ten Troughs Development Company,'" Ames read dryly. "It's all right. I never expected it to read the Great Western Dam and Be Damned to You Company."

"Hardly." Waranrode smiled. "My lawyer got another lawyer to incorporate with an out-of-state capital subscription, and with a board of directors who are nonentities. I don't see why my name should ever be connected with it."

"There's Trueblood's paper there."

Waranrode said gently, "Yes, Trueblood."

"He's got a long nose," Ames said, watching Waranrode carefully. The senator did not rise to it, and Ames asked gently, "How much longer do you aim to put up with him, Matt? He's rawhided you these five years in that paper of his." Still Waranrode said nothing, and Ames stilled the fire of his discontent in his eyes, but not before he added the warning: "You let him snoop around much more and he'll have the whole thing printed."

Waranrode savored the rich smoke of his cigar for a moment, then said, without looking at Ames, "You took a long chance and it turned out a mistake, Ames. Let me take one on my own hunch."

"What long chance was a mistake of mine?" Ames asked.

"Putting Pete Yard to guard Trueblood."

Ames flushed. "All right. That was a mistake, maybe. But I reckon I fixed it."

"You think Yard will leave the country?"

"If he doesn't want the same thing over again, he will. And I don't think any man would want that again."

Waranrode said nothing.

"What long chance are you goin' to take? Let Steve Trueblood snoop?"

"Exactly."

Ames regarded his employer with a hard and speculative

gaze and then he drew out a sack of tobacco dust and rolled a cigarette. Presently he said, "I've worked for you for fifteen years, Matt. You're a gambler in some things, but not where your reputation is at stake. Whatever you're goin' to do now, you've misnamed. It isn't a long chance, or you wouldn't take it."

Waranrode allowed himself a thin smile. He said, "Suppose I let Trueblood alone. What will he do?"

Ames thought a moment. "Likely he'll go up to the north Basin and organize those ranchers to fight Ben Mellish. When he does that, and if they listen to him, Ben will come out in the open with his fight. After that, every acre of land that Ben gets for you will cost him a month's wages for a gunhand. I doubt if Ben could do it."

"There'll be open war, then?"

"Certainly."

Waranrode regarded the cigar in his thin fingers. "What if Steve Trueblood is killed in this war?" he murmured. "It might be handy, mightn't it?"

"Handy for who?" Ames said quickly. "You let him organize these ranchers and then put him out of the way. The harm will already be done, Matt."

Waranrode rose and walked over to the fireplace. There was wood laid, and he kneeled down and touched a match to it. Watching it catch, he said mildly to Ames, "Have you any idea how much money I have, Ames?"

"No."

"Several millions. Do you think I'd risk my reputation as a senator, risk everything I own for a few thousand more—the few thousands I'd get from selling that Basin land to Eastern farmers on a part-time plan?"

Ames scowled at him for a long moment. Then he uncrossed his legs and recrossed them the other way and lit his cigarette again and said humbly, "Why, damn me, I did. I'm wrong, then?"

The senator nodded and turned his back to the fire, which was burning brightly now. It gave the room an air of added richness, so that the blaze played a sheen on the walnut bookcases. Pleasurably the senator clasped his hands behind his back and teetered a little, as a man naturally does. His face, which in middle-age had been thin and keen and almost predatory, had settled into something resembling benevolence, and it seemed relaxed and kind as he inquired mildly of Ames, "That calendar on the desk, Ames—what date does it show? The twenty-fourth?"

Ames corrected him. "The twenty-fifth."

"On the third, next month," the senator began, "that's Monday—a man in the department of Indian Affairs will arrive here from Washington. He'll have a letter from Senator Crippen of Delaware, who is chairman of the Committee on Indian Affairs. It will be the usual letter, asking me to show this man all courtesy. After he's settled, Ames, one of my men will act as his guide. He'll go to the Ute reservation and talk with Major Linkman and the Ute chiefs. We won't be included in this parley because the session will be secret. He'll do a lot of riding, most of it at the east end of the Ute reservation, and he will request me to have my men keep his movements strictly confidential. Do you follow that?"

"As far as it goes. What's behind it?"

Again the senator smiled. "I am. I have been for three years. It's cost me in the neighborhood of a quarter of a million dollars, paid out mostly to our esteemed senator from Delaware."

Ames was scowling, puzzled.

"You see, I first had to bribe Senator Crippen of Delaware, then jockey him into the chairmanship of the Indian Affairs Committee." He added dryly, "It took some planning."

Ames was still scowling.

"To return," the senator said. "One of the first bills passed by Congress in this last session was one designed to reduce reservation lands where they are in excess of the actual needs of the Indians." He paused. "Does it begin to make sense?"

"No."

"Consider these Utes here. Ten years ago their herds

were twelve times what they are now. At present the government is having to feed them, and it's sick of it. It's building this dam, which will provide water. It aims to irrigate land for the Utes and induce them to farm and support themselves. Once that's done, they won't need near the reservation land they've got. So the government will cut it down, putting it up for public sale."

"And that's what this Washington man will do here—decide what lands should go?" Ames said slowly.

"With the aid of Major Linkman, who is my partner in this business, he will. Yes."

Ames said more slowly, "Linkman, eh? Let's hear the rest of this."

"With the invaluable aid of Major Linkman, who should know the needs of the Utes better than any man," the senator continued dryly, "the Washington man will recommend that the block lying between the Raft River and Lowenweep Breaks, from the Ute Lake east to the badlands of the Walking River, be put up for public sale."

"That's a big chunk," Ames said cautiously, "and not good range."

"Think."

Ames shifted in his chair and took out his sack of tobacco and rolled a smoke, not looking at his hands, watching Senator Waranrode.

"I got part of it," he said presently. "Last year you bought the Chevron from Lassiter and that blankets the Lowenweep Breaks."

"So no one will have access to this block from the south. Go on."

"And you hold a mortgage on the Schumacher boys' place, which runs from Ute Lake to the badlands. That blankets the north side of the block."

"So the two logical bidders for this block of reservation land will be Schumacher and Lassiter—and they'll each get a half."

"Bought with your money and then deed it to you?" Ames asked, beginning to understand.

"Exactly."

Ames thought a moment. "I've seen a lot better range."

Waranrode said dryly, "So have a lot of people, thank the Lord, so there'll be little bidding competition. But what neither you nor they have seen, Ames, are the thousands upon thousands of tons of coal on the badlands edge of that block."

"But it's a hundred miles to a railroad," Ames said, frowning.

The senator said, "But it will be less than a mile when the railroad builds up to it—and past it on north skirting the edge of the badlands into the rich ore country to the north."

"But will it?" Ames said quickly.

"Senator Crippen seems to think so," Waranrode said gently. "He and his family control the board of directors of the transcontinental to the south. The spur is already projected. All that remains is a choice of route, and Crippen will decide that. And when he does, it will be found that the railroad has to deal with Senator Waranrode for its coal, just as the mines and towns to the north will."

He spoke it mildly, but he was watching Ames, and quietly enjoying the look of amazement on his usually unreadable face. Now he threw his cigar in the fire and sat down in the easy chair beside the fender and continued to talk.

"So that is why Trueblood should be encouraged in this noble work of uncovering speculation behind the Antelope Butte dam. It's for the public good and I commend it highly. Of course"—and here his voice slipped into iron sarcasm—"if Stephen Trueblood should have the misfortune to be killed by parties unknown in this Ten Troughs war, the state and nation will have lost a powerful newspaper crusader. I will even send a letter of condolence to his family."

Ames looked at his cigarette a long time and when he raised his gaze to Waranrode his eyes were filled with an indolent sheepishness. A slow smile broke over his face. "Matt," he said humbly, "you reckon you've got an old ribbon around here I could wear in my hair? I am not only not growed up, but I suspect I've been impersonatin' a man with brains."

Waranrode smiled. "Since a dog has never been known to dig out a badger who has two holes to his burrow, we'll let Trueblood whet his appetite for scandal on that Ten Troughs fraud. It will afford perfect cover for this bigger scheme. And when things get warm over there, the world will lose Trueblood." He paused, then added quietly, "At last."

He was silent then, enjoying the homage paid him by Ames. It was tonic and reassuring, evidence that the years had dulled neither his wits nor his imagination. But lest he should seem too proud of this, he did not dwell on it long, for his sense for theatrics was as much a part of him as his cunning.

"This Pete Yard," he said. "I'll take your word for it that you can run him out of the country."

"Only that? He knows as much as Trueblood."

"But he hasn't Trueblood's public conscience," Waranrode pointed out. "Right now, Trueblood is almost sure I'm behind Ben Mellish. But there's no way to prove it, and he knows that if he spreads this around without proof, I'll smash him. So he won't tell the Basin ranchers about me, because all he will want of them is to fight, and they have their enemy in Ben Mellish. Trueblood will wait, trying to get his proof against me—and he never will. Yard is different. Knowing just as much as Trueblood, he will do nothing. He's a puncher, with a puncher's brains, and he knows what he's bucking." He added decisively, "Yes, another beating will drive him off, if he's still there."

"Don't make a mistake about this Pete Yard," Ames warned him. "I know him."

"So do I," Waranrode said curtly. "There's no necessity of doing any more than scare him."

Stubbornly, Ames had his mouth open to protest when the sound of footsteps in the corridor outside closed his mouth. To the knock on the door Senator Waranrode said, "Come in." The door opened and Sylvia Waranrode entered. She nodded to Ames and strolled over to the fire, touching her father's shoulder as she passed him.

"You sly devil," she said to him and laughed. She had an easy, languid grace in her walk that the wine-colored silk evening dress did not hide. She stood facing the fire, hands outstretched to its warmth, watching him, a look of mild vexation on her dark, modeled face. Ames was already standing. He said now, "If that's all you want, Senator, I reckon I'll go."

"Don't go, Ames," Sylvia drawled. "I want you to hear him crawl out of this."

"Out of what?" Waranrode growled fondly.

"You left me with him on purpose," Sylvia accused. "Am I supposed to tolerate all the windiness of a set of Blackstone just because you're in politics, Dad?"

"Send him packing," the senator said. "He's a bright boy with a future, though."

"As a mesmerist, perhaps," Sylvia said, with a touch of her father's irony.

"I've done that for him all my life, Miss Sylvia," Ames drawled. "I remember the time he asked that bird collector out. For two weeks I did nothin' but tote a picnic basket and binoculars and it rained every day. Your dad caught a bad cold the first day and couldn't stir out of the house—until after we'd left."

The senator smiled. "That's what you get for being dull wits. I think of an excuse first."

Ames grinned and picked up his hat. "I'll say good night to you."

When he was gone the senator observed his daughter more openly. Her dark skin, almost foreign-looking, reminded him of her mother, for whom he had sent back to Tennessee when he was settled here. Two years of its remoteness had killed her, but her daughter seemed made of sterner stuff. Her dark, wavy hair was her mother's, and that proud mouth that seemed a little arrogant until she smiled. Perhaps school in the East, from which a month ago she had returned, was a respite from this lonely country that she needed and that her mother had lacked.

So he asked curiously, "Glad to be back?"

"You know I am."

"Find it dull after the East?"

Sylvia shook her head and laughed. "I didn't—until you took my guide away from me."

"Who was that?"

"Pete Yard. I liked him."

"He's a puncher, Sylvia," the senator said. "If I kept him at riding with you, he'd soon ask for his time. Besides, you don't need one. You've grown up on this place and should know every inch of it."

"When you add a thousand acres every year?"

"Still, it's a working ranch, dear, and I can't interfere with Ames's men. If you want a man to take you hunting and fishing and riding, I'll ask Ames to lend you another man, a—a less valuable one than Yard."

"But I want him," Sylvia insisted, smiling a little. "He doesn't mind."

Waranrode looked up quickly at her. "Did he say so?"

"No. But I could tell."

The senator shook his head. "He's busy. Someone else, perhaps, if Ames agrees."

For a moment neither spoke, and then Sylvia said softly, "Where is he, Dad?"

The senator only glanced at her and then drew out a cigar and lighted it and afterward said casually, "I don't know. Isn't he here?"

"He's been gone a week."

"Probably at one of the line camps, then. It's time to move the stuff up to summer range, and all hands are needed."

"But he isn't," Sylvia insisted. "When I ask any of the men they just shrug and won't talk—or they make up a dozen lies that don't agree."

The senator said brusquely, "You've inquired for him, then? From the men?"

"Yes."

"I wouldn't do that," Waranrode said gravely. "It's hardly wise."

"Why?"

"Because—because they might get the wrong impression, is all."

"That I like Pete Yard?"

"Yes."

"But I do."

This time Senator Waranrode's glance was shrewd, less gentle, revealing a hardness that he did not often let Sylvia see. "Like him?" he echoed. "How?"

Sylvia laughed a little. "Like I like a man that's good at anything. He's good at his business, Dad. More than that, he knows this range. I remember once we sat and watched an old mother silvertip teaching her two cubs to fish for trout. They spoiled two pools for her by their playing until she had to cuff them quiet. When she finally flipped out a big rainbow, it landed in front of them. They just sniffed it and walked away. It made her mad. She— Why, what's wrong, Dad?"

Senator Waranrode had risen out of his chair, and his face was angry.

"Silvertip—with cubs!" he said angrily. "Is the man a fool? Doesn't he know they're positively savage in spring!"

"But he had a gun and he wasn't bothering them. He—"

"Nonsense!" Waranrode said curtly. "If I could ask Ames to let him off, I certainly wouldn't now."

Sylvia approached him and laid her hands on his shoulder. "Why, Dad. I've never seen you so angry. What's the matter?"

The senator contrived a smile, and patted her arm affectionately. "Nothing. Only I distrust a man who takes needless risks. Your Pete Yard is such a man, and you'll not see him again. You understand?"

Sylvia bowed her head in mock humility. "Yes, O iron parent," she said, but beneath her levity was a wonder at her father's anger over something that was at bottom trivial. And his evasiveness, for not even now did she know more about Pete Yard's whereabouts than when she first asked.

Waranrode said gently, "We've a guest downstairs, dear. Windy or not, we have to entertain him. Come along."

That night, when the house was quiet, Waranrode sat alone in his study, recalling what Sylvia had said of Pete Yard. It seemed that Ames had got this young man out of the way just in time to stop Sylvia's infatuation with him. Waranrode pondered darkly on this for a few moments, but slowly all thoughts of Pete Yard faded from his mind, supplanted by something closer to his heart. Tonight he had laid before Ames all his ambitions and plans for the future, and he felt almost empty, drained of emotion. And yet Ames had not been told all of it. But perhaps Ames could see what had been left unsaid, that when this plan was consummated it would only be the beginning. By these vast coal fields a city would spring up—a Waranrode-owned city. Mills, factories, maybe his own railroads, would follow inevitably, and they would be Waranrode-owned. Some day, perhaps in his own lifetime, he would look upon the rounded empire he had dreamed of in his youth. History would not forget him along with a dozen anonymous Western senators; it would remember him in the same thought with the Eastern financiers as a man who had helped build a nation, a man of power. And between him and this stood only an inquisitive newspaper man and a forty-a-month cowpuncher. They hardly deserved the honor of being called his enemies.

But before retiring Senator Waranrode made his way over to Ames's stone quarters, which were not far from the bunkhouse. The upshot of this visit was that Ames received more definite instructions as to Pete Yard. No, Ames was not to kill him, but he was to make absolutely certain that the G.W. had seen the last of him. Absolutely.

CHAPTER FIVE

It seemed to Chris that the very fact she had offered to nurse Doctor Benbow's patient had made that nursing unnecessary, for the morning after the night she arrived the man announced to her that he wanted to get up.

Discreetly she laid his breakfast down and said, "I'll ask the doctor after breakfast."

Feeding only irked him. He said, "I can use my hands. Why am I wrapped up like a mummy, ma'am?"

"I'll ask the doctor. Now take this." She fed him awkwardly, while he, restive under his outward calm, eyed her in silence. She knew he felt embarrassed at being treated like a child, and his embarrassment was contagious. She was feeding him some thin soup, and when it was gone she said, "Enough?"

"Of course not."

She laughed a little and stood up. Somehow this made her feel superior to him, better able to face his inquisitive stare. She wished she could see beneath the bandages to his face, for she was certain she could face him more easily then. Now he was only a hulking figure in this bed, and a gruff, petulant voice. Last night he had listened to Doctor Benbow's account of where he was, how he had been found, and to what the trouble was with him. Doc had introduced her after that, and he had looked at her searchingly, as if he might know her or had at least heard of her. If he understood her name he never repeated it, and he did not volunteer his own. He also got the gun he demanded and put it under his pillow. All during the evening he had watched her until, long past midnight, her weariness conquered and Doc told her to go back to her hotel room. He hadn't wanted to talk; he seemed only to want to look at her. And right now, with the empty dish in her hand, he seemed to want the same thing.

"I'll get some more," she said hurriedly, flushing a little.

"Don't bother."

"But aren't you hungry?"

"Yes, ma'am."

Chris frowned at him and said, after a moment's pause, "You don't like this?"

"No, ma'am," he said flatly.

"What would you like?"

"Something to eat."

Chris smiled at this and had her mouth open to speak when he drawled, "You'll ask the doctor," mockingly. "All right. Go ask him. Bring him in here."

Doctor Benbow was eating in the kitchen. He came in, napkin still tucked in his vest.

"What do you want?" he asked bluntly.

"Something to eat."

Doc went to the door and called to Mrs. Carew. "Bacon and eggs and coffee and lots of it, Mrs. Carew." He turned to the man again. "Anything else?"

"I'd like to get up."

Doc looked at him with amusement in his eyes, but his face remained grave. "All right. Go ahead." He didn't move. Chris watched the man as he struggled a moment, lifting his head; and then all the anger that had been pent up in him burst. "Damn it, Doc! Get these rags off me! Let me sit up!"

Doc laughed, and Christina did, too, although her laughter was a little hysterical. She was used to rough ways, having been raised with two brothers, but this transition was too sudden. Doc, however, seemed to accept it. He went over to his bag in the corner, brought out the scissors, and said to Chris, "You go out and let him dress."

"But—" Chris got out, and then saw the look in Doc's eyes and understood. Doctor Benbow's treatments had always been unorthodox. This was one of them. Chris went out.

Doc advanced to the bed and threw the covers back. He snipped the bandages binding the chest and the arms and then stepped aside and said, "All right. Sit up if you can."

Slowly the man raised himself to a sitting position. Doc heard his breath catch, but that was all. Once erect, Doc said, "Now I'll take those off your head and face."

This took more time, and when it was finished Doc grunted with satisfaction. From the waist up the man before him was bigger than Doc remembered, with a deep, broad chest capped with thick ropes of muscles. The chest and shoulders still bore the fast-healing marks of the whip. The head sat squarely on the shoulders, and for the first

time Doc got a normal look at the man's face. It was
marked with bruises, but the lips of the wide mouth were
nearly natural, then. The nose was still taped tightly
across the bridge, but it would have been aquiline; and
the cheekbones were high and rather prominent, so that
the eyes were deep-set. The left one was still discolored
and almost closed, but the right one looked at Doc with a
vast impatience. His black hair was short, almost wavy,
stiff and yet not coarse, and it clung to the clean line of
his head.

Doc said judiciously, "You didn't look that good in bed.
How's your back?"

"All right."

Doc backed away. "Stand up."

It took a moment of effort for him to swing his feet out
of bed. Not wanting to bind his back, Doc had not put a
nightshirt on him, but had left him naked from the waist
up. Below he wore a pair of Doc's linen pants, sizes too
large at the waist, inches too short in the legs. As he planted
his feet on the floor the legs of the pants came scarcely
below his knees.

"You'll make it," Doc said gently, dryly, too.

Pete Yard heaved himself to his feet, and for a moment
he swayed there, towering above Doc, while his face
drained of color. Doc didn't move to assist him, only said,
"Try to walk."

Pete Yard, trousers gathered in one hand at his waist,
took two steps, paused, swayed, and fainted.

Chris heard him fall, and she rushed into the room. He
lay stretched out on his face, full length, while above him
Doctor Benbow considered him musingly. The napkin
was still tucked in his vest. He looked up at Chris, smiling
a little. "You know, I'm hanged if he didn't get halfway
across the room."

They got him back in bed, and Doc went out to finish
his breakfast, as if nothing had happened.

But if Pete Yard missed being a well man, he was on
the mend, and considerably chastened. Doc's demonstra-
tion had been more convincing than advice, and he was

content to spend part of the day in bed, silent and brooding. Chris began to think he did not like her, for his lean, bruised face never lost its somberness, and when he spoke it was curtly, with a kind of smothered wrath. His gestures were quick and alert, but his inability even to roll a cigarette for himself bred such an impatience in him that it was communicated to Chris, and she drove herself into fumbling and clumsiness.

When she could stand it no longer she went to Doc and told him she wanted to leave, but he would not listen to her.

"But, Uncle Doc," she protested vehemently, "he doesn't need me. If I roll a hundred cigarettes for him and put them on his table, my work is done. He sits up. He reads. He walks a little. He's dressed. He could come to his meals, and in a few days he'll be fine. He's no trouble."

Doc pushed her down in a chair and stood before her. "All that's true," he said, "but finish the picture. You're watching a man who's playing a game—a serious one. He's crowding himself, and more than a man should. An ordinarily healthy man would take a month before he'd venture to stir from his bed. It's been how long?"

"Five days?"

"Five days. He sits there in that chair by the window, thinking up ways to punish himself. When he should be resting, he's trying to walk, and cursing because he can't. When he should be sleeping, he's awake and resting for strength. The only sane thing he does is eat. He's got that much animal in him."

"But make him stop it!" Chris said.

"Do you think I could?" Doc countered.

Chris thought a second and said, "No."

"Neither do I. One of these days he'll put on his hat and walk out of this house. I hope he does before it happens."

"What happens?"

"I don't know. Whatever it is he's waiting for," Doc said slowly. "Maybe he can do it. He's tough. But if he can't— if some day he just caves in, he's going to need attention and need it quick. That's why you're here." He smiled at her now. "Besides, it's lonesome here for him. He likes your company."

"He does not!" Chris contradicted him. "He tolerates it—and barely."

"You stay," Doc said.

Mrs. Carew had only part-time work here, so that she was gone a good part of the morning. If Doctor Benbow was going to be home for lunch, she came over. If not, she did not return until time to cook his supper for him. So Chris, whether she liked it or not, was with Pete Yard a good deal. Now that he was up and dressed most of the day, she spent much of her time in the other part of the house, but she would look in on him occasionally and find him at the window which looked out on Doc's tiny garden. He never spoke, only regarded her somberly, as if she were a stranger.

Once, looking in this way, she found him standing beside his chair regarding the gun Doc had given him. He looked up at her and made a motion to hide it, and Chris said, "I've seen it. Don't you remember? I gave it to you."

"Yes."

Chris smiled sympathetically. "Now that you aren't having nightmares, why don't you put it away?"

"It wasn't a nightmare," Pete Yard said quietly. "I'll be leaving soon."

"Suit yourself."

That night Doc had a call to an outlying ranch to attend a woman in childbirth, and for the first time Pete Yard ate at the table with Mrs. Carew and Chris. His face looked weary and drawn, but the swelling in it was gone, and the bruises were gradually fading. That morning Doctor Benbow had removed the bandage from his nose, and now Chris saw what he truly looked like. His face seemed leaner now, and more tense, with a kind of hard wariness that made him seem reckless and somehow handsome.

During the meal Mrs. Carew mentioned that a cousin was visiting her, so when the meal was finished Chris insisted on Mrs. Carew leaving the cleaning up for her to do, which that prim woman reluctantly consented to.

After she was gone Chris prepared to wash the dishes, while Pete smoked in moody silence at the table.

When she was ready to wash she suddenly found him standing at her side, a dish towel in his hand.

"It's about time I started earnin' my keep," he said, with a crooked smile. It was the first time Chris had seen him smile, and she looked down at her hands in haste, to hide her surprise and confusion. "All right."

They had just begun when the knob of the back door made a small noise. They both looked up to behold Big Ben Mellish step into the room, Ames Manderfield behind him. Ames held a gun in his hand, but it was not pointed at anything in particular. He gave a swift glance at the room and then he closed the door and leaned on it, saying quietly, "Hallo, Pete."

"Ben," Chris said quietly.

She felt Pete Yard's hard rough hands on her upper arms as he moved her to one side of him and laid his towel down on the table.

Ben Mellish looked at Pete, as if sizing him up, and said over his shoulder to Ames, "Do you think he can stand it?"

"I don't know," Ames said mildly. "Can you, Pete?"

Pete was scowling, nothing more. He said mildly, "Short of shooting, I can stand most anything."

Ben said, "Clear out of here, Sis. Get on the other side of the table."

Chris didn't move until Pete said, "Go ahead, Miss Mellish."

Slowly, her face white with fear, Chris backed around the table toward the door to the bedroom, while Ben said to her without turning, "You've just begun this nursing job, Sis."

He walked forward, arms at his side, his massiveness dwarfing the room.

Chris understood fully then, and she cried, "Stop, Ben! He's been sick!"

"He'll be a sight sicker," Ben murmured.

Pete Yard made a small, unnecessary gesture of hoisting up his trousers and waited, and Ben, smiling darkly, reached out a ponderous fist to gather in his shirt front.

The move was casual, and before it was completed Ben struck out with his other hand, driving it at Pete's face. Chris saw Pete's hand chop this blow short and then there was a slight weaving of his torso and she heard the sharp crack of knuckles on padded flesh. Ben staggered back, but it was all so quick she did not follow it.

Ben, cursing in his throat, rushed in now and they were locked in each other's arms, feet planted, bracing them, their shoulders corded and taut. Chris heard the floor creak and the sharp gusts of their breaths as they exhaled. Ben's huge arm was wrapped around Pete's neck, and he turned slightly and thrust his shoulder under Pete's chin and heaved, trying to break him over backward. Chris thought of that healing back, and she wanted to cry out; and then she understood Ben's aim. The two men were rooted there by the hot stove, and Ben was struggling to bend Pete over onto its hot top. Chris screamed and then it died as she watched.

She heard Pete's strangled laugh, while Ben, body rigid in this labor, left the floor a few inches as Pete twisted his head out of the crushing pocket of Ben's elbow. And suddenly they were parted, but Pete had hold of Ben's one wrist, while Ben had hold of Pete's other. Ben's face was purple with the effort, but there was a puzzled look in his baleful eyes as he regarded Pete, whose face was white as lime and smiling.

"Maybe you'd like that," Pete said softly between his teeth, and started to force Ben's hand down toward the stove top. Ben braced himself and heaved and then his jaw muscles started to cord and the two were almost motionless. Ben struggled like a man bound in iron, but slowly Pete was forcing his hand down, and the veins in his temple began to swell until they seemed ready to burst. And still Ben's fist drew nearer the stove. They were staring at each other now, as if trying to will each other to defeat; but as Ben's shoulder sloped down Chris heard a savage growl well up in his throat.

And then she looked at Ben's hand. It was unfisted now,

fingers outspread in a kind of frantic shrinking as it was forced inexorably down, down. And then Ben made the mistake of shifting his feet, and the hand settled abruptly on the stove top. It was there long enough to make a dull sort of bubbling noise before Ben's cry filled the room. Pete, still smiling, stepped away from him. For a moment Ben swayed there, looking down at his half-raised hand, and then he turned and with a torrent of oaths picked up a chair and swung it over his head. It crashed down on the chair which Pete had managed to lift in front of him. In panic, then, Chris ran into the bedroom.

For the first time there was anger in Pete Yard's face—stark, insane anger. As the force of Ben's blow with the chair was spent, Pete laid a hand on it and the wrench he gave it brought it out of Ben's hand and crashed it against the far wall. Pete was close now, and viciously, savagely, he drove swift slogging blows, one fast on the other, at Ben's face. The first was enough. Ben's arms seemed aimless, flailing the air, and then they fell and Pete Yard hit him so that he was driven into the stove, to carom off it limply and sprawl on his back on the floor.

Ames Manderfield looked down at him and made no move to raise his gun when Chris's voice lifted in the silence. "Don't move!"

Slowly Ames swiveled his head to confront the gun Chris held in her hand. In time she had remembered it was under Pete's pillow. Now she held it steady, cocked, trained on Ames Manderfield.

Ames only regarded it with a casual glance and turned to look at Pete Yard, who was standing with legs outspread, breathing deeply and wildly.

"We made a mistake, Pete," Ames said mildly.

"It'll take a better bully boy than that," Pete agreed.

Ames looked down at Ben, who rolled over now and slowly pushed himself to his knees, shaking his head with dogged insistence; and then he looked up at Pete and said, "Not next time."

Pete Yard said nothing.

"Get out of here, Pete, while you can," Ames said

mildly.

"No more buckos?"

"No more buckos. Do what I say."

Ames holstered his gun and helped Ben to his feet, opened the door, and steered him out into the night, closing the door after him.

Chris leaned against the wall, limp, watching Pete regard the door with a contained thoughtfulness. Wearily, draggingly, then, he walked over to a chair and slumped into it and put his face in his hands.

Chris put the gun down and walked over to him and he raised his head. "Thank you," he said, and then he said more softly, "I'm tired."

Chris said quickly, miserably, "You're hurt. You—" And then she suddenly sensed that pity would be an insult to him, and she broke off, and said more calmly, "But why? Why did they come? That—that was my brother Ben."

"I know."

"You, too."

She, too, sat down now across the table from him, listening to his labored breathing, understanding nothing except that the hand of Ben's violence had reached down here to him. The memory of his savage anger still frightened her, so that she sat utterly motionless, the color beginning to creep back into her pale face.

She heard him say, "I'm sorry about that. For you and Doc, I mean. I knew it was coming."

"Why did you?" Chris asked suddenly, and before the veil of secrecy could again come into his eyes she asked, "Haven't I a right to know? Ben is my brother."

Pete said gently, "I was a traitor. That's a traitor's medicine."

"A traitor to Ben?"

He shook his head. "No. A little Lord God over yonder," he said with quiet bitterness, dragging himself to his feet. Erect now, he looked down at her and his face held a strange gentleness. "I wonder," he said slowly.

"What?"

"Why you did that—why you got that gun. At the time it seemed right. Now it only seems queer." He hesitated.

"Why did you? He meant to shoot."

"You were sick," Chris said swiftly. "Besides—whatever Ben does is wrong! I felt it!"

"You know that?" Pete murmured.

"I left my home because of it."

Pete raised a hand and stared wearily at it and then he let his arm swing down to his side and looked levelly at her. "You are going to be hurt," he said evenly. "Why don't you get out of here? Go anywhere."

Chris only shook her head, but she was watching him, trying to understand the meaning behind what he had said.

"What you did tonight was brave. But it will take a different kind of bravery from now on to face what you will have to."

"I think I've had a taste of it," Chris said quietly, and then she added swiftly, passionately, "If I only knew what I was fighting! Why is it happening? And what is happening?"

She caught a look of almost pity in his eyes as he turned away and walked into the bedroom. At the door he paused and put a hand on the jamb and looked over his shoulder at her. "Maybe I can pay this back to you and Doc—but to you especially."

A moment later, hearing no sound from the room, she rose and looked inside the door. He was spread-eagled out on the bed, his face buried in the pillow, deep in a sleep of exhaustion.

Then he, too, like Doc, like Ben, like all of these people around her, was not going to tell her what it was she was living through, she thought. But she felt, without knowing why, that Pete knew better than the others whereof he spoke, and she was almost afraid.

CHAPTER SIX

ED BRIEDEHOFF'S PLACE was not exactly small; its bare living-room was ample enough to hold all these men. But they declined to gather there and chose the porch instead. It was not strange to burly Ed Briedehoff, smoking his pipe in the doorway with the light of the lamp behind him, that these twelve men chose the friendly dark, for it was easier to meet trouble in the open—and safer—when you were not among friends. Their horses were not in Ed's corral, but tied outside to the poles of it, as if the owners did not intend to stay long. And Ed was as skeptical as the next man of this night's meeting.

They sat on the edge of the porch, feet on the ground, in little silent clusters of two and three along the length of it, the occasional glow of their pipes and cigarettes flushing the night. Ed was a neighbor to most of them, unfriendly to half, hostile to the rest; but he regarded them with an easy tolerance tonight, for something was in the wind.

Swan Ullman asked from the darkest corner, "You sure it was tonight, Ed?"

Ed had the light on him, so he only nodded.

Swan said, "I can think of a lot of reasons why a Mellish-owned sheriff would call us together, but none of them reasons are any good."

"You can go, if you want, Swan," Ed told him quietly. "Nobody made you come. Nobody'll make you stay."

"Is that why Lockhardt never come?" Swan asked.

"He was asked. He didn't come. If you don't want to stay, you can go," Ed repeated.

Swan rose. "I reckon I will," he said soberly. "It don't take a long head to guess what Nance wants. He'll warn us is all."

"He wouldn't come out here just to say that," Ed said.

"Whatever he wants, tell him my vote's 'No,'" Swan said grimly. He walked off in the dark toward his horse, and Ed Briedehoff watched him with neither pleasure nor anger. None of the others commented. But the fairness that was part of Ed and which gave him a normal desire for peace told him that unless he did something now, Sheriff Ross Nance's meeting would never come off.

So Ed spat out onto the hard-packed dirt where the light cast its clean rectangle and said, "No offense to Swan's friends, but that was a damn-fool thing for Swan to do."

"How do you figure that?" a challenging voice said presently.

"Nance wants to tell us somethin'."

"Maybe you know what it is, Ed," this same voice said accusingly.

Ed only shook his head. "I've got no love for Nance. My place happened to be the closest to the rest of you. I don't know what Nance wants, but I do know he won't ride out here to threaten us. He'd be afraid to."

"He'd better be," someone else said.

And no one moved to follow Swan, but Ed wondered how much longer they would wait. He was still wondering it twenty minutes later and with increasing anxiety when someone announced, "There's someone."

Two men got up and went out to the corral, and Ed could hear the greetings given. Presently they all returned, and Ross Nance greeted these men from the dark. The replies he got were civil enough, but lacking in warmth. He walked up onto the porch, so that he was in the square of light. There was someone with him, Ed noticed, but it was too dark to see and Ed turned.

"Maybe we better talk inside," he said, and there was a general movement along the porch.

Ross Nance followed Ed into the bare room, which held, besides a table on which the lamp burned, several benches, some rickety chairs and a trunk. The floor was littered with riding-gear.

Sheriff Ross Nance was an old man, a little hunched,

with a permanently fretted expression on his settled face.
The first signs of that shrinkage of flesh that comes to an
old man could be seen about his neck and jowls and hands,
for he seemed to have too much skin for the body of him.
But his hair was black and thick and his eyes were keen.
He stood perhaps six inches less than the man following
him, who wore a careless black suit with trousers tucked
deep into boots, and who could have been half the age of
the sheriff. This man looked around the room and then
traded his amiable stare with the dozen men who tramped
in behind him and found seats. His hair was very light,
long, after the city fashion, strangely in contrast to his
large, homely, wind-reddened face. Of all these men he
seemed the best-fitted by nature for an open life, and yet
his clothes, his pale hands, and his white shirt announced
him a townsman. There was a kind of clumsy and gangling
grace about him as he moved across the room and sat on
the lone window sill while the others found better seats
and removed their hats, or shoved them back off their
foreheads.

Ed Briedehoff waved his pipe at Nance and said, "Here
we are, Ross. What is it?"

Nance nodded toward the stranger. "This is Steve Trueblood. Most of you read the *Enterprise*. He owns it." While
the others regarded Trueblood with impassive curiosity,
Nance went on. "It's no secret there's trouble in this county. Trueblood wants to talk about it."

"And tell us to clear out and leave the Basin to Ben
Mellish?" one of the men asked bluntly. Nance shifted his
eyes to regard the speaker.

"I don't know," he said levelly. "I didn't ask him. Maybe
you better had."

Trueblood lounged to his feet and crossed to the table
and leaned on it, turning down the lamp wick a little so
that the light would not be so strong in their eyes; and
while he did it he said in a low, resonant voice without
looking at anyone in particular, "I just had a few things
to add to that write-up about the Antelope Butte dam—
things I couldn't print."

It was a matter-of-fact announcement, almost casual, but he had calculated that it would jerk the attention of these suspicious men, and it did. They were a rough lot, he saw, men without many possessions or much money, the kind of proud men he understood and loved without being sentimental about it. He had their attention now, and he said, "It's the kind of a thing a newspaper can't print without having the proof, and I haven't got it. But it's true, and since you're the men most concerned, I reckoned you should have it."

He looked at them, his eyes suddenly alert and his voice a little louder. "This is a plain land steal," he announced. "The Mellish boys are behind it. I don't have to tell you that."

"That," Nance said grimly, before anyone could answer, "is a damn lie!"

Ed Briedehoff's square face shifted into a dour amusement. He touched Ross's arm and said, "You brought him out here, Nance. If he don't dance to your tune, let him talk anyway."

Nance shook his hand off and said to Trueblood, "If you come up here to stir up more trouble, you can leave."

"He'll stay," Ed said briefly, flatly. "He'll talk, too, if it means we gag you, Nance." To Trueblood he said, "Go ahead. He'll be quiet."

The sheriff settled into a surly silence, and Trueblood went on calmly. "Six months ago I heard about this trouble starting, and I made a trip up here to look this Basin over. The reason I did was because Dave Mellish used to say to my father that it would only be a matter of time before the Utes here were turned into farmers." He paused. "That's a queer thing to start a man's curiosity, but it started mine. Believing that, and knowing that a man can't farm unless he has water when he wants it, I thought I saw what the Mellish boys were driving at. They wanted to get the land and water rights along the Ute River and they didn't care how. You know that now, don't you?"

"I reckon we do," one of the men said dryly.

Trueblood nodded. "Then I sat down to think, like a man will, and I figured that the Mellish boys must know that a dam was being planned. I didn't know how they knew it, but I was pretty sure they did."

"How did they?" Miles Leston asked.

"I don't know. I will before I'm through, though," Trueblood said quickly, flatly. "But to go on. I started to worry the War Department at Washington. I asked them if a dam would be built here at Antelope Butte and when." He smiled. "All the answers I got were the same. The Department was not authorized to make a statement. So last week I made a statement on my own hook."

For a long minute the men looked at him. Finally, Ed Briedehoff said, "That article in the *Register*. You made that up?"

"I did."

"Then it ain't true?" Ed said.

Trueblood grinned. "After I wrote that article and it was printed, I telegraphed it clean to Washington—all of it—to the War Department. Three days later I got back the answer. You'll read it in next week's *Register*. Except for a change of words, it announces exactly what my article did. It forced them to come out in the open with it, just as I hoped it would."

There was some grinning among these men, because this was their own way of playing a game, and they approved of it. They approved of the man who worked it, too, for the tension and the suspicion in the room were lessening.

"I did something else, too," Trueblood continued. "Last week at the capital I found that a new corporation had been chartered. The name of it is The Ten Troughs Development Company. It's the corporation that holds all the land the Mellish boys have stolen and claimed and bought; and its stockholders are out-of-state people." He paused. "That's what you men are bucking."

This news was met with grim silence, but Trueblood needed no one to interpret it for him. Men brought out smokes now, and the matches flared around the room. It was Ed Briedehoff who said finally, "They're payin' Ben Mellish and his riders?"

"Maybe not. Maybe they're just buying the land Ben gets."

"It amounts to the same thing, don't it?" Miles Leston asked.

Trueblood nodded, but said nothing. He wanted these men to turn this idea over and arrive at their own conclusions. And it was Ed Briedehoff who spoke first again. "If I believed what you wrote in the *Register*, I reckon Ben Mellish did, too." He looked at these men. "It don't seem that Ben's through yet, then."

Someone said then, "No, only today he rode over to Swan Ullman's with five men. He told Swan it was time to sell."

They nodded, and now they looked at Trueblood again.

"He did the same thing with Pax Luffler," Ed Briedehoff said grimly. "Pax left. So did Amon Rinker. Lee Moorehead wouldn't move, and Frank Mellish is dead." He looked at the others. "Maybe he won't be so gentle with Swan. Maybe he won't be with the rest of us when we tell him we won't move off our land."

"Have you got that land surveyed and recorded?" Trueblood asked quietly, and not a man in the room said yes. "Then he won't be gentle with you," Trueblood said briefly. "You'll get what Pax Luffler and Rinker and Moorehead got, only worse. And when you're driven off your land you'll find you have a battery of lawyers and court summons and bribery and lying witnesses to fight to get it back. Because you're not fightin' Ben Mellish; you're fighting a company with money."

Sheriff Ross Nance's voice whipped in on the echo of Trueblood's talk. "If there's a fight in this Basin, Trueblood, I'll have you arrested for incitin' to riot and for the accessory to every murder that happens."

This time Ed Briedehoff lounged off the wall and stretched out a hand to whirl Nance around to face him. "Ross, get out of here. Everyone knows Dave Mellish gave you land and cattle and a sister for a wife, but he never gave you the pair of blinders you've been wearin'. Now get out and tell Ben Mellish about what we know now."

Nance settled a baleful stare on Trueblood for a long minute, then wheeled and walked out of the room. Miles Leston, a middle-aged man in clean, oft-washed clothes, cleared his throat now in the following silence. Somebody looked at him, and it encouraged him to speak. "What do you suggest doin', Trueblood?"

"Fight," Trueblood said curtly. "Organize and fight."

Before anyone could speak he raised his hand and said, "I know what you'll say. There's hard feeling between almost every man in this room. That still doesn't change it. If you want to stay here, you've got to fight."

He lounged to his feet now and reached for his hat. "That's all. The rest you'll have to work out for yourself. I've told only the truth."

Miles Leston slipped out with him and they walked over to the horses in silence. When Trueblood was mounted Leston said quietly, "We're obliged for this. Maybe your trip wasn't wasted."

Trueblood laughed gently. "They'll wonder," he said. "They'll think I've something behind all this I want to get. Tell them I have. Tell them I'll get it, too. But tell them if they want to be here to watch me get it, they'll have to fight."

"What is it you want?" Miles inquired.

Trueblood didn't answer for a moment. Then his voice was quiet in the night. "A long time ago this country was clean and its men couldn't be fooled. I want to get it clean again, that's all. Because all the pirates didn't sail the seas. Tell them that. Good night."

Miles stood there a moment, until rider and horse blended with the night, and then Miles returned to the room. It was quiet; no one talked, and Miles slipped into his seat.

Ed Briedehoff knocked out his pipe onto the floor. "Well," he drawled, "you believe what's before your nose now?" He glanced around at them and caught Cass Ford's meditative stare upon him. "You, Cass. Which would you rather fight—Ben Mellish or your neighbors?"

Cass's drawn face flushed a little. His outfit, right under Antelope Butte, was the best situated in the valley, and he was the most independent of these men. His small, hard-bitten face settled into grimness as he leaned forward, elbows on knees. "Now that you've called for plain talk, Ed, I'll give it to you. In the twelve years I've been here I've had to ride line summer and winter, and I've still missed beef. Not a neighbor of mine ever shared a day's work with me. Not a one of their womenfolks ever helped my wife when her kids came. I've took care of myself and mine. I reckon I can keep on. And I don't reckon I give a hootin' damn what happens to the rest of you." He rose and picked his way through the men and walked out.

Barney Newcomb, one of Cass's neighbors, rose and said as he pulled down his hat, "I don't, either, Ed. I'd sooner fight Ben Mellish than ride with this outfit."

After Barney went the meeting broke up. Ed made no attempt to hold it together, for he knew these men too well. He only observed dryly before they left, "We've all agreed on one thing, that this Basin has been too crowded for five years runnin'. In a month it won't be near so crowded."

Miles Leston stayed behind. Together, out on the dark porch, they watched the riders scatter and ride away.

"That," Miles observed, "puts it up to each of us."

"Maybe it's better that way," Ed murmured. "Except for you, Miles, I kinda feel about the rest like Cass does."

CHAPTER SEVEN

EVEN IN DAYLIGHT Steve Trueblood had a hard time finding the creek and then the fork of it that Pete had named a week ago as their meeting-place, so that it was past full sunup before he rode into the clearing among the lodgepoles where Pete was camped. But the fire was dead, and

Steve looked around. Off near the brush he saw a figure bundled in blankets, and he dropped the lead rope of the pack horse and dismounted. Standing over Pete he regarded the bruised and scarred face with quiet amazement, and then he stuck out the toe of his boot and moved it gently into Pete's stomach. Pete wakened immediately and sat up, and Steve observed dryly, "Who was right?"

Pete said, "Right?" not understanding.

"Remember we saw a little bit of each other a week ago?" Steve said in broad sarcasm.

Pete did. For three days he had guarded Trueblood at one of the G.W. line camps, held him as a prisoner of Waranrode. "A little. Why?"

"Remember when you turned me loose you had the gallant notion that you ought to ride back and tell your friend Ames Manderfield what you'd done?"

Pete nodded, looking up at him.

"I observe by your face that you got the welcome I predicted you would."

"Oh," Pete said, and threw the blankets from him. He reached for his boots and said, "Two of them—with a third promised."

He told Steve about the flogging and Ben Mellish's attempt to improve on it. Steve watched him fondly, and when he was finished and had gone to the stream to wash, Steve smiled grimly and went over to build up the fire and start breakfast. He was not surprised at Pete's news, for nothing about Pete or his actions was orthodox—not even his first meeting with him.

That meeting had occurred at Toolle, a cattle-shipping town a hundred miles to the south, where Steve's newspaper was. He had been working late that night in his office, and he had thought himself alone. Somebody coughed behind him, and Steve had whirled to confront a cocked gun in Pete's hands. Pete had said quietly, "You work too hard. Come on and take a rest." That had been the kidnaping, as brief and final as the spoken words of it.

Ames and Pete took him to the line camp of a ranch. Steve didn't know what line camp or what ranch, but he gathered from the conversation of his captors that they were Anchor riders, working Ben Mellish's will. At the time that made sense to Steve, for he had broadly hinted in a newspaper story what he was almost certain of, that Ben Mellish was behind the Ten Troughs trouble, and that speculation was his motive. Later, when he was left alone with Pete, he found that Pete knew nothing of the reasons for the kidnaping. It had taken three days of sharp and weary argument to convince Pete that these reasons were true; and then Pete, in turn, had told him Waranrode had ordered the kidnaping, not Mellish. And it had been ordered for only one reason, that Waranrode was afraid Steve might, in casting about for the source of the Antelope dam leak, light on Senator Waranrode before his mind was made up as to Mellish's guilt; or so Steve and Pete reasoned.

And from that hour on they had been friends. Pete had left to confess his treachery to Waranrode, Steve to write his bluffing editorial that had brought the Antelope dam affair into the open, and to try to organize the ranchers of the Ten Troughs Basin against Mellish.

When the hot bread was shuffled out of the skillet and served up with the bacon and coffee and they had eaten their fill, Pete settled back on his haunches and rolled his smoke.

"Any luck with the ranchers?"

Steve told him of last night's events. "But they're an independent crew, people say. We'll see." He packed his pipe and lighted it. "If it takes, we'll be in trouble before we leave here. We'll need a place that isn't known."

"There's an abandoned line shack up in the mountains over on the Bar Stirrup range," Pete said. "We can use that."

"I thought you didn't know this country," Steve said.

"I've made friends," Pete answered laconically. Once mounted they worked up through the timber using trails when they could, and while they rode they discussed the possibilities of Mellish winning. It was then Pete asked, "Did you tell them who was really behind this land steal?"

"I said Mellish," Steve told him. "It's the only lie I told."

Pete rode on in silence for a long while and then he said suddenly, "If Waranrode gets this Basin land, what will it amount to in money?"

Steve looked swiftly at him. "A hundred thousand dollars. Hardly that."

"Does it strike you funny," Pete murmured, "that a man with a couple of million is willin' to risk a Senate seat and his reputation to get a few thousand more?"

Steve smiled faintly, as if to himself, and looked obliquely, curiously, at Pete. "You tell me," he said slowly. "I've fought him for five years and I still haven't got his measure."

"Does it?"

"No."

"Then why is he doin' it?"

Steve didn't know, and he said so.

They nooned late, ate a quick meal, and pressed on. The timber was smaller here, and the country rougher and more canyon-shot. The air still held the chill of snow as it beat off the close peaks now. Doc Benbow had told Pete of this place, describing it as best he could, and Pete was feeling his way, watching for the landmarks named. He was ahead now and it was past midafternoon when he pulled up and regarded the ground.

"Tracks?" Steve asked.

Pete nodded and looked off toward the south. They were on the hump of a ridge whose sides were steep and comparatively treeless, so that Pete could catch a glimpse of a small grassy park below them and to the south.

"Over there's the shack," Pete said. "Looks like somebody else had heard of this, too."

Dismounting, he kneeled and touched the tracks, then rose and followed them off the ridge into the tangle of scrub oak below.

In ten minutes he returned and said to Steve, "Two Indians with two pack horses. They've been huntin', I reckon, because there's blood on the brush. One of them's a woman."

Steve said dryly, "Was she walking?"

"No."

"I suppose you can tell she's a woman by the tracks her horse makes?"

Pete grinned. "Did you ever see an Indian hunt without a woman? Somebody's got to do the work."

"That means our shack is taken, then."

"I don't reckon," Pete said. "I never saw an Indian sleep in a shack when he could get out of it. They likely spotted that grass and camped there for horse feed. To-morrow they'll drift down lower and make a meat camp and dry it before they head for the reservation."

"You're going to risk someone knowing our camp, then?"

Pete looked up the slope in the direction from which the tracks came. Timber line was in sight now, and beyond them were the sparse boulder fields and then the snow. He said softly, "I wonder."

"What?"

"Those Utes have got to have permission to leave the reservation. This range here is Bar Stirrup's, but it's leased to Ben Mellish, I've heard. And I've heard tell, too, that these reservation Utes won't hunt on Mellish range now that the old man is dead."

"What are you getting at?"

"This. Either they've been hunting on Anchor lease land with Ben Mellish's permission or else they've come from over the mountains."

"Over the mountains? I doubt it. But what of it?"

Pete said quietly, "That's G.W. range over there."

Steve repeated, "What of it?"

"Come along," was Pete's only answer. They kept to the ridge until they came to a spur of it, followed it out and down into timber and then into a grassy *cienega* several hundred yards wide.

They could see the Indians' camp now, and they rode across the park toward it, Steve watching Pete's face. The line shack lay at the head of the park, a log affair with a sod roof, but the Indians had ignored it. Four paint ponies grazing toward the edge of the *cienega* looked up at their approach and watched them cross.

A fire was going now in the Indians' camp. The buck was in the midst of constructing a wickiup of pine brush, but he ceased when the woman called to him.

As they approached, Pete said, "I know him. It's Stumbling Bear, a Ute subchief."

Steve said nothing till they rode into camp. Stumbling Bear was a young buck, tall, slim, and had the typically full Ute face, with its thin nose. He was dressed in worn buckskin trousers which were wet and clung to his legs, and a cast-off army short coat. His black hair had buckskin braided into it and hung down on his coat lapels as he walked out to meet them.

Pete greeted him familiarly, and Stumbling Bear returned the greeting, smiling a little, while his wife poked the fire and kept her eyes down. She was young, dressed in bundlesome calico and beaded moccasins and short cloth coat. Around her the clean grass was littered with bloody elk meat which had been boned to facilitate packing it.

Stumbling Bear was introduced to Steve and then he and Pete had a few words of conversation in Ute, while Pete rolled a smoke and offered the Indian his tobacco sack.

Then Pete turned to Steve, who had been listening blankly.

"He says to eat with him tonight. There's a brisket boiling."

Steve grinned. "Why not? He knows our camp already."

"But they won't have it out of him," Pete said strongly. "He's a friend."

It was arranged that Steve should take their pack over to the shack, rustle wood, and turn the horses loose while Pete helped with the wickiup, and Steve left, wondering what was behind Pete's decision.

Steve did more wondering that night as they ate and afterward when they were stretched around the crackling campfire. Steve had seen Utes, had known many Indians.

There was always a kind of veiled indifference in their eyes when they had contact with a white man. He had seen old Indian traders converse with them in their own language and come away in a fury at their feigned stupidity. The usual parley consisted of the white man talking, the Indian smoking, shrugging, answering in monosyllables, or remaining silent altogether; but what he was seeing now was different. Stumbling Bear talked gravely, occasionally laughing, listening to Pete's rapid Ute with respect. The wife, across the fire and withdrawn from it, watched Pete with curious, live eyes. Occasionally, out of politeness, Pete would turn to Steve and translate the conversation. It was trivial, dealing with hunting mostly. Stumbling Bear had shot five elk. He was taking home all the tongue, briskets, kidneys, back-fat, and boned hindquarters he could pack. Stumbling Bear offered Pete a hindquarter, which was accepted without further ado. The remainder of the meat was cached and would be hauled when Stumbling Bear had more time, Pete said.

"Where is it cached?" Steve asked curiously.

"Over the mountains. On G.W. range," Pete said, grinning a little. "Stumbling Bear had Waranrode's permission to hunt there. He gets it every year in the spring when food's a little short and they're sick of army rations. He's in a hurry to get home now."

"Why?"

"A meeting of all the chiefs and subchiefs. He stopped at Waranrode's and there was a man from the Father in Washington who told him to go back to the reservation for the meeting this week."

"Translate that," Steve said dryly.

"Waranrode's got an Indian agent from Washington staying with him. He'll have a parley with all the Ute chiefs this week sometime."

Steve received this without comment. "Ask him what the meeting is for," he said.

Pete did. Steve watched Stumbling Bear's face, and he thought he saw a look of contempt in it, but his speech was as measured as it had been. Pete listened gravely, his dark hair glinting in the firelight. He had been playing idly with a knife, but now his hand was still. When Stumbling Bear was finished, Pete turned to Steve and said, "Do you want a free translation of this, or an exact one?"

"Free?"

"Well, these double-damned, blasted fools in Washington who have let the white man forbid the Ute to hunt are now trying to turn his people into Hualpais, he says."

"What's the matter with the Hualpais?"

"He doesn't know. His father and his father's father told him about them. They are people to the south in the dry country who live in mud houses and raise brush to eat," Pete said, laughing quietly. "In other words, the pueblo farmers that the Utes used to raid."

"Why don't they ranch, ask him."

Pete was facing Steve fully now. "I did," he said, and paused a moment. "When I tell you this, I don't want you to act surprised, because Stumbling Bear will notice it and wonder." He paused again. "They don't ranch because there's not enough land," Pete said slowly. "He knows there won't be enough because the agent has told them that the Father is going to take some of their land away from them, that they don't need it all to farm on."

Steve nodded idly, his face impassive. "And where is this land they're taking away?"

"He doesn't know. He doesn't even know if it's so. Maybe that's what he'll find out next week." Pete smiled faintly and turned to Stumbling Bear. The rest of the evening was spent in idle talk, in yarning, none of which interested Steve.

Later, after Pete had made a gift of several sacks of tobacco in exchange for the gift of meat, he and Steve mounted their horses and rode across the park toward the shack. The stars were semaphoring silently overhead and the breeze riding down off the mountains was cold and keen.

They did not talk for several minutes and then Steve said, "Why did you tell me not to show any surprise at what Stumbling Bear said?"

Pete laughed quietly. "Because an Indian—any Indian —will tell you anything if he thinks you don't care about knowing it. They're the greatest gossips in the world."

"I didn't mean that. What was there in what he said that I'd be surprised at?"

He could almost feel Pete's eyes on him. "Were you surprised?" Pete countered.

Steve waited a moment before he answered. "Part of the Ute reservation is going to be cut off. The agent is staying at Waranrode's," he mused. Then he asked, "Is this supposed to be a secret among the Utes themselves?"

"Until it goes through."

"Is it customary for a visiting agent to stay at Waranrode's?"

"This man is special, I guessed. Not the regular inspector."

They rode on, hearing the heavy swish of the lush grass as their horses pushed it aside.

Presently Steve said, "I'm suspicious, maybe. But look. It could be, couldn't it, that Waranrode wants a slice of this Ute range?"

"It would be put up for public sale."

"Damn you," Steve murmured disgustedly.

They were at the shack now and they unsaddled and turned their horses loose. Inside, with a candle lit, they investigated their quarters. Two bunks, a crude table, and corner fireplace of mud and rock built up off the floor. Steve set the candle on the table and looked steadily at Pete. He was glad of the light now, so that he could watch Pete's face. He put his dry pipe in his mouth and sat down on the edge of the bunk.

"Remember, we both thought it was queer that Waranrode would risk this Basin scandal for the little money to be got out of it?"

Pete nodded.

Steve said, with oblique reasoning, "Did you ever hear of the old outlaw trick of starting a fire on the edge of town so they would draw the crowd away from the bank they wanted to blow."

"The dam, the Basin war, being the fire," Pete murmured. "All right, where's the bank?"

"A chunk of Ute land."

"Put up for public sale," Pete reminded him, and shook his head. "Waranrode is always after range. But he can only get this land in one way—by biddin' against other men at public sale."

Steve started to speak twice and closed his mouth each time. Pete was busy with the bedrolls. When the two bunks were filled with new brush, Pete sat down and drew off his boots. Steve did the same. Then, finished, they faced each other a moment. Steve shook his head and there was a scowl on his homely face. "It made a hell of a good story," he drawled. Pete grinned at him and blew out the light. There was a long silence then, and Steve did not hear Pete turn over in readiness for sleep. Presently he said, "Pete," and Pete answered.

"Is Stumbling Bear coming back after the rest of the meat?"

"As soon as the parley is over."

"Will he come this way?" Steve persisted.

"I reckon."

It was a little while before Steve asked this next question. "Will he tell you what they decide at the meeting? What piece of reservation is to be sold?"

"If I ask him."

"Will you, then?"

Pete said, "It's no good. We're wrong, no matter how much we want to be right."

"Will you?" Steve insisted.

"All right."

Steve sighed. "All right. Tomorrow I leave."

Pete didn't say anything for a full minute. Then he asked, "For good?"

"Don't be a damn fool," Steve drawled sleepily.

CHAPTER EIGHT

FOR FIFTEEN MINUTES after Sheriff Ross Nance left the
Anchor with a solid breakfast under his belt, Ben Mellish
remained in the big room of the house, turning over in
his mind the news Nance had brought the night before.
The Basin ranchers were organizing—and against him,
Nance believed. He smoked one cigarette after another.
Occasionally he would pause in front of the big fireplace
and stare balefully into its glowing coals, only to rouse
and throw his huge bulk into a chair. The way was clear
to him. The thing to do now was to bring this war out
into the open. He was organized, had absolute command
over his crowd of fighting men, and the sheriff was sym-
pathetic. The thing to do was strike, while it was still time.

But whenever he thought of this he remembered Ames
Manderfield's orders: "Don't stir up trouble without telling me." But Ames had also said, "Don't ever come over
to the G.W. One slip that way and the whole thing will
come down on our heads." In other words, he was to wait
here until Ames gave him further orders. Which might be
a week.

Ben was half in the mind to go ahead on his own initia-
tive, for these last two days had not been pleasant ones
for him. His left hand was swathed in bandage, and each
time he forgot and was reminded of it by pain he thought
of that night at Doctor Benbow's and he had a feeling of
savage humiliation. But it did not make him so angry that
he lost sight of the risks in this game he was playing. Still,
any repression always galled him, and this was repression.

He left the house and walked out to the corrals, restless,
impatient, knowing with a kind of cross-grained stubbornness that he was helpless to move.

A couple of riders were hazing the *remuda* into the
corral, and Blake, the foreman Ben had substituted when

Dave Mellish's foreman quit, was sitting atop the corral poles. He was a quiet man, who never spoke of himself, and who had a way with the riders. He had been recruited a month ago down south when Frank had made his trip in anticipation of trouble. Spare, wiry, with a reticent respect for his employer, he was nevertheless a driver who had backed up his orders the first week at the Anchor by pistol-whipping one of the new hands.

He greeted Ben with a curt nod and watched the horses milling around in the corral. A half-dozen hands were inside, waiting their turn with ropes to snake their mounts for the day. They greeted Ben and got a scant nod in return.

One of the riders now rode over to Blake and said, "That G.W. bay is in the bunch again, Blake."

"I thought I told you to lose him," Blake said, letting his gaze rove the *remuda*. The bay was there, all right. Four days ago they had found him running with a bunch of the Anchor horses, and, at the orders of Blake, who was an eminently cautious man, he was cut out and driven off.

"When was this?" Ben asked sharply. He had overheard.

"Four-five days ago."

Ben had a swift recollection of something Ames had casually let drop. Ames had said he and two of his men had followed Pete Yard across the mountains, caught up with him, flogged him, and delivered him to Doc Benbow. Ames had never said so, but Ben guessed that Ames had thrown Yard's saddle in the brush and turned his horse loose. This bay would be Yard's.

"Why wasn't I told?" Ben asked.

"I reckoned you'd want me to do just what I did," Blake replied, without looking at him. "Trouble's easy enough to start in this country without you're accused of stealin' a horse."

Ben glanced swiftly at him, but Blake's face was bland and unreadable. Ben knew Blake had seen Ames Manderfield's horse on one of Ames's visits, and he would be a strange cowman if he had not noticed the brand; and then he understood this was Blake's way of telling him that he understood enough of the part the Great Western Cattle Company was playing in this business to know that secrecy was imperative.

Ben smiled slightly, regarding the horse, a big-boned, deep-chested bay. And then Ben knew that his mind was made up, that he was going to take things in his own hands.

"Saddle him," Ben said. "I'll be over south for a few days. I'll go out of my way and drop him on G.W. range."

Blake turned his head and looked at Ben. "And walk back?"

"I'll get a horse from the Ute agent," Ben said impatiently. "That's who I'm seeing."

Blake said to the rider, "Cut him out and saddle him."

Ben felt better now, as a man always does when he has made a decision. He rolled a smoke and then gave Blake his instructions, as if he had been planning this for a long time.

The instructions were simple enough. Blake was not to take the men off the ranch under any provocation. Blake understood, and within fifteen minutes Ben was riding the bay away from the Anchor.

To Big Ben Mellish, who was not an imaginative man and who had never been above timber line of the Raft peaks, there was only one way to the G.W. So it took nearly three days to ride south to the lower spurs of the Rafts, where he crossed over and came back to the Great Western headquarters.

From far across the plain Ben could make out the buildings of the Great Western under the spread of cottonwoods shades lighter than the green of the pines on the slope behind it. He studied it with growing interest as he drew nearer.

Riding into the plaza below the house, a gust of the spring wind stirred a banner of dust before his horse. He pulled up, regarding the place with hardheaded approval. Two punchers were cajoling a skittish bronc into the wide door of the blacksmith shop, while the blacksmith himself stood at the door, arms akimbo, for a spell of the clean and wild air. He paid no attention to Ben until, after pulling his horse over and beside the shop and laying both square hands on the horn, Ben inquired of him, "Where will I find Ames Manderfield?"

The blacksmith told him civilly enough that Ames was gone and would be for several days.

"Then is Senator Waranrode in?" Ben asked.

This time the blacksmith looked at him again and said, "You'll have to find that out at the house." He waved a grimy hand toward it, and Ben rode on, through the rough plaza past the bunkhouse on across to the log watering-trough which paralleled the low wall enclosing the house.

Ben dismounted stiffly, letting his reins trail while the horse drank, and passed through the gate. His scowl appeared now, for he had a notion of what Waranrode would say to him.

Sylvia was seated in a deep chair on the porch. Her book lay idle in her lap and she was watching three pups as they romped in snarling abandon around her feet. Her face was unsmiling, pensive, until she heard the heavy tramp of Ben's boots on the thick flagging and turned to see his heavy, dusty figure approach. She caught in an instant that this man had ridden hard. His bold and sullen manner told her, too, that this was his first visit, and that he was a stranger to the deference men paid her father. His left hand, she noticed as he removed his gloves, was bound in dirty bandage, and it had been long since he shaved.

Ben paused near her. "Is Senator Waranrode in?" he demanded brusquely. Sylvia did not answer immediately, only regarded him with immediate and ungentle dislike.

"It's Ames Manderfield you want," she told him.

"He's not here, I was told."

Sylvia said, "No, he's not," and waited for Ben to go on. He shifted uncomfortably. "Then I'd like to see the senator."

Sylvia's impulse was to be rude, a thing this man contrived to do without seeming to, but instead, she rose and went into the house, Ben behind her. He followed her trim figure, dressed in riding-clothes, half through the long hall and upstairs into the corridor.

Sylvia knocked on the study door, and when she was bid enter she turned and left Ben. He opened the door and stepped inside.

They had never seen each other, Ben and the senator, yet Waranrode seemed immediately to know him, Ben saw. He was at his desk, deep in the correspondence which Sylvia would help him with that night. The trim tweed suit and shoes seemed strange to Ben, who had known other Western senators and found them little different than himself.

Waranrode said coldly, "I thought you were told not to come here, Mellish."

Ben nodded surlily and said nothing, and Waranrode indicated a chair, which Ben took. He laid his hat and gloves on the floor, as if he intended to stay.

"What is it?" Waranrode asked.

"Where is Manderfield?" Ben said bluntly. "Have I got to wait for him before I move?"

"What is it?" the senator repeated.

"Trueblood has organized the Basin ranchers," Ben said hotly. "While I'm waiting word from you, I've lost the chance to break it up. Where is Manderfield, I say?"

The senator was no stranger to this strategy of cloaking guilt with aggressiveness, and he did not propose to pretend he was; and he said coldly, "I've hired you, Mellish, and I expect obedience from the men I hire. I thought you understood that."

"You expected results, too, didn't you?"

"I did."

Ben's head was a little bent, as if he were glowering, and he said sullenly, "You'll not get them this way."

Waranrode toyed with a paper knife, openly watching this huge man of whom Ames had talked much and with contempt. He said suddenly, "What did you come over here for, Mellish?"

"Orders. Since you won't bring them to me."

"Is that all?"

Ben laid a huge flat hand on his knee. "Now that you mention it, no." His scowl deepened. "You can't run it this way, Waranrode. Either put Ames over at my place and give him my men or let me run this."

Ben was prepared for almost anything as he said this. He had understood from Ames that Senator Waranrode was a man who brooked little contradiction, usually because his own judgment was so good. But Ben had already borne enough humiliations to risk his anger, and he waited.

Surprisingly, Waranrode did not immediately answer, as if he were giving it some thought. Then he shrugged. "Why not? The time for caution is past."

Ben stirred in his chair, feeling his point won.

"What do you want to do?"

"Keep my word," Ben said grimly. "I promised Swan Ullman I'd be back in a week to get his answer. That week will be up when I get home. If I had made it three days instead of a week, what would I have done?"

"You'd have run him off, probably," Waranrode said, and smiled a little. Ben accepted this tribute to his stubbornness without a smile.

"You want to run it your own way?"

Ben nodded faintly, emphatically.

"How?"

"I've got a third of the Basin already by playin' these men against each other, by buying, and by showing I meant what I said." Ben tapped the gun at his hip. "This has always talked louder than a man's voice, Waranrode. We've got to face it. We fight now, and the outfit that strikes hardest and oftenest and quickest is the one that'll win. I've got Nance behind me. Give me a free rein and I'll swing it."

Waranrode, nodding absently, rose and crossed to a deep leather chair by the fireplace, where he was in shadow and Ben was in the full light from the window. "That's very good," he said mildly, as he sat down.

"Another thing," Ben went on stubbornly. "About this Pete Yard. I want him out of the way."

"Is he still in the Basin?" the senator asked quickly.

"I don't know. From what Ames says and—and from what I've seen of him, I reckon he is. Trueblood is not a fighting man. Someone will lead those men."

"And Pete Yard will do it if he's there," Waranrode said gently. It was not a question, merely a plain statement of fact, and it stirred some deep satisfaction in Ben when he heard it.

"I'll get him out of the way, too, if you give me a free hand," Ben said.

"If I wanted to make a mess of this, I can't think of a better way to do it, Mellish," the senator said dryly. "Trueblood is fighting for an abstract principle now. Kill Yard and he'll be fighting for a concrete one—damned concrete."

"But not if it happens my way."

"And what way is that?"

Ben stared into the shadow trying to make out Waranrode's face. Then he said, "My brother Frank was killed there in the Basin two weeks ago. Two of my men know how it was done. It wouldn't be hard to convince Nance that they saw it done—saw Pete Yard do it." He paused. Waranrode said nothing. "It wouldn't be hard to put five thousand dollars on Yard's head. Once that was done, Pete Yard would turn up dead or alive—but he'd turn up."

Waranrode was utterly still.

"Because," Ben pointed out gently, "there's not a nester in that valley that wouldn't turn in his brother for five thousand dollars. If Yard is turned in dead, it's not our doing. If he's turned in alive, well, no jury will doubt the word of my men." And he added grimly, "At least, they'd better not."

Waranrode said quickly, "What's he done to you, Mellish—this Pete Yard?"

Ben's face flushed deeply, from neck to forehead.

"I don't mean that fight," the senator said. "That could happen to anyone. I could have told you it would. But why do you want him out of the way?"

"Comin' from you, that's queer," Ben drawled quietly. "If you'd had the sense two months ago to do what I'm suggestin' now, maybe I wouldn't be suggestin' it."

Waranrode smiled at this and stood up and walked over to his desk. "All right. Put the five thousand on his head. It's you who'll be fighting him."

"That's what I thought," Ben said grimly.

Waranrode sat down now at his desk.

"Anything more? Do you need money or men?"

"No. I need a horse. I rode Yard's over."

Waranrode scribbled something on a slip of paper and gave it to Ben, saying, "Give this to Martin, the horse wrangler." He looked directly at Ben now, and Ben understood from that hard and unbending expression that up to now Waranrode had been almost tolerant. "Understand this, Mellish," the senator said gently. "I won't have any more of your coming here. To all purposes, we've seen the last of each other. You're hired to obey my orders. See that you do it."

Ben flushed angrily, but Waranrode had already dismissed him with not so much as a handshake or a curt nod.

Sullenly Ben swept up his hat from the floor and went out. Halfway down the stairs he remembered his gloves, which he had laid on the floor under his hat. Paused, he was almost in the mind to go back, but when he recalled his dismissal he turned and tramped stubbornly down the stairs. He had no stomach for more of Senator Waranrode. Besides, he won what he had come for.

Outside he even smiled at his success. The porch was empty. He walked its length and saw that Sylvia Waranrode was sitting on the low wall beside the watering-trough.

She was stroking the nose of the bay when he came up to her.

"Don't I know this horse?" she asked, looking at him with more friendliness than she had shown before. Ben inclined his head and said, "Very likely. He's a G.W. pony."

"Pete Yard's, isn't it?" Sylvia asked, studying the horse.

"I wouldn't know," Ben said with caution. "I found him on my range."

Sylvia shifted her glance to him, mild surprise in it. "But that's quite a way, isn't it?"

"The Anchor, over on the west slope of the Rafts."

"And what about Pete?"

Ben shrugged, watching her closely, seeing the frown crease her forehead.

"That's strange," Sylvia went on. "Something must have happened to him." She hesitated. "Did you tell Dad about him—about the horse, I mean?"

"Yes."

"What did he say?" Sylvia demanded quickly.

Her curiosity about Pete Yard irritated Ben, and he remembered her father's jibe of a few minutes ago. Waranrode—and now even his daughter—seemed to have an exaggerated respect for Pete Yard. Ben smiled, narrowly watching Sylvia's face for any change of expression as he said, "He was glad to get the horse back. As for Yard, I'm afraid he won't be back. You see, he has a price on his head."

Sylvia's face was suddenly still. "Is that why he left here?"

"No. He just acquired it—the price."

"For what?"

"Murder."

"That isn't so!" Sylvia said swiftly. "Where?"

"Ten Troughs County."

The color drained from Sylvia's face. She rose and walked to the house without another glance at Ben, who watched her curiously with cynicism in his eyes.

CHAPTER NINE

ED BRIEDEHOFF was an observant man, already versed in the lessons those around him were having to learn. So when the rider appeared suddenly from the fringe of pines down the slope that ringed the shoulder of the knoll on which Ed's place was built it was only a matter of seconds before Ed saw him. He let go the stiff hide he was cutting thongs from and walked leisurely to the house, snapping his knife shut and ramming it in his pocket.

At the doorway he paused and leaned against the jamb, first glancing inside to make sure the carbine stood within reach. Then he regarded the approaching rider. While packing his pipe with stubby, grimed fingers, Ed played his usual game and lost, for there was nothing about the set of this man in the saddle, about his horse, about his rig that told him anything. Ed's grimness lightened a little as he flicked a match to pipe and settled his burly shoulders and waited.

The rider walked his horse into the hard-packed circle of dirt before the porch, and in that brief instant which cattleland takes to size up a stranger before speaking, Ed saw that the horse had been recently run.

"Mornin'," Pete said.

"Mornin'," Ed replied noncommittally. He did not append an invitation to alight, and Pete did not seem to expect it.

Pete said in a voice almost as casual as Ed's, "I saw Ben Mellish and five of his riders take the road over to Swan Ullman's."

Ed removed the pipe from his mouth with a deliberate gesture and spat clear of the ten feet of porch. "That so?" he said amiably. "How long ago was that?"

"Ten-fifteen minutes."

Ed was noticing several things about this stranger which gave him pause to reflect. First, the man had been in a fight recently, and still wore the marks of it. Second, he had a gun rammed in his belt, which argued either that he had only recently acquired it or that he wore it holsterless because it could be unlimbered faster. "And I'll bet he's knocked the sight off it," Ed thought, as he looked at the man's face again. Certainly it was a face primed for trouble, lean, expressionless, a trifle hard, and with a sleepy alertness in the eyes.

Ed said slowly, "What's that to me? Or to you?"

The stranger took a deep breath and shook his head. But he changed his reins from his left hand to his right, a concession to caution, and ran his left hand, palm down, along the slope of his leg, wiping it dry of perspiration. "Depends," the man said. "Trueblood said to let you know."

Ed's eyes narrowed and he shuffled his boots a little so that the sound of them was loud on the boards, and then quiet settled.

"Trueblood," Ed repeated, and Pete nodded.

"I don't recollect he mentioned you," Ed continued. "Fact is, I don't recollect your name."

"You never heard it," the man said. He gathered up his reins. "I'd guess there'd be a short cut to Ullman's up this way. Is there?"

Ed didn't answer immediately, and when he did it wasn't properly an answer. "Swan wasn't here that night. It wouldn't of made much difference. Nothin' came of the meeting."

"That's a pity," Pete mused.

"It just didn't work."

"A pity," Pete repeated. "If that place of his ever got into strange hands, it might make trouble for the folks downcreek from it. Prior water rights and such." He straightened up. "About this short cut."

Ed's face betrayed a little of the surprise he felt at this statement coming from a stranger. Pete waited courteously.

Presently Ed said, "I'm downcreek from him. I guess it sort of puts it up to me, don't it?"

Pete said nothing. Ed went into the house and came out with a shard of mirror. Stepping out into the sun and holding it chest-high, pointed down valley, he murmured, "Miles is downcreek, too."

"I wouldn't bother," Pete said. "We don't have the time."

Ed looked across the long sweep of valley. Below him,

in a tiny clearing among the pines, he could make out Miles Leston's place. This crude heliograph might summon Miles, but it would take time for him to get his sons and ride up. "Hell," Ed said mildly.

"We better hurry," Pete said lazily.

Ed knocked the ashes from his pipe and put it in his pocket. "You might be one of Mellish's riders for all I know," he said, still looking down into the valley.

"I might," Pete conceded. "Maybe you can find out."

"How?"

"By seeing what Mellish says to me."

"It would be too late then," Ed said.

"That's right."

Ed looked up at him to see if the face held the same dry dare the voice did. It did, and anger stirred in Ed but he said with patience, "If what you say is true, Mellish would have passed Miles's place."

"He didn't. He did travel trails this time."

"And how do you know that?"

"Because I've been watchin' the Anchor for three days." And then he said gently, "About this short cut?"

Ed didn't answer. He went to the door and lifted out the carbine and went over to the corral. In a moment his horse was saddled and they cut in between the house and the corral and took to the trees on the up slope.

Presently Ed said, "It'll sound funny for me to make a threat."

"Go ahead."

"If you've tolled me up here to get me off my place, or to give Ben Mellish a crack at me, I'll gut-shoot you, sure as hell. Surer than hell."

"All right," Pete said.

Ed picked the way up the slope, slacked off the line of the ridge into a narrow valley whose bottom was surprisingly free of brush, took a feeder canyon a mile above it to the right, made his slow way up the face of a hogback, and reined up on the top. They could see a log shack off to the far side of the valley beyond. Ed watched it for several seconds. A woman came out the door, sloshed a pail of water out into the brush, and went in again.

Ed grunted and put his horse down the slope. In another five minutes they walked their horses into Swan Ullman's clean and hard-packed yard. Swan greeted them from the door, and it was much the same greeting that Ed had given Yard.

"Better get your woman out of there, Swan," Ed said, looking around him. Before Swan could answer, Ed said, "She can take our horses over in that wagon shed."

He dismounted then, Pete doing the same thing. Swan Ullman walked over to them, his rifle in his hand. He was a spare, faded man with straw-colored hair, and he had a kind of implacable truculence in his manner and his talk as he said, "What kind of damn nonsense is—"

"Ben Mellish," Ed said curtly. "Get your wife."

For a moment Swan only stared at him and then he turned and called over his shoulder, "Emma!"

His wife must have been listening, for she was already out of the door before Swan had called her.

"What is it, Swan?" she asked, her voice no stranger to trouble. A fretted, work-worn, and unlovely woman, she stood among them in a brightly clean dress and looked from one to the other, and finally her gaze settled on her man.

"Mellish," Swan said. "Take them ponies over and put them in the wagon shed. You stay there, too."

She took the reins from Ed and Pete and walked the horses across the bare corral lot. Swan led the way into the house. Inside it reflected a proud, neat poverty; and a tin can holding fresh blue columbines sat on the sill of the open window, pert flags of defiance.

Swan's hard, suspicious glance shuttled from Ed to Pete. "How many of them?"

"Five," Pete said.

Crossing to a wall shelf, Swan reached both hands up into a wooden box and ladled down cartridge shells to the table. Pete stood in the doorway, looking down the valley, and he could almost feel Ed Briedehoff's eyes at his back. They would be unyielding, withholding judgment; and probably they would not concede the inquisitive Swan's right to ask questions until this was over.

Pete half-turned and said to Ed, "Here they come. Five, besides Ben."

"Ah," Ed said, looking at Swan, who picked up his rifle and stepped past Pete out in front of the door.

Ed said, "Maybe you better go out with him."

"I want to hear Mellish," Pete murmured, not looking at him. "I want to hear how he says it. Likely it won't be the last time we'll hear it."

"Not from behind my back, you won't."

"No. You stay there. I'll stay here."

Ed didn't say anything, but he didn't move, either, and the sound of the approaching horses came to them. Presently it was close and then it ceased, among a jingle of bridle chains. Swan was standing with feet spread a little, holding his gun in both hands.

Then Ben Mellish's deep and wrathful voice came to them. "Swan, I told you to be out of here by today."

"So you did," Swan said mildly. And then his voice lost all its mildness. "First one of you gets off his horse will have to be helped back on."

Ben Mellish's voice said, "Blake, drive off those ponies in the corral and fire that shed."

Pete stepped swiftly out the door. The six riders were ringed in a loose half-circle confronting Swan, perhaps twenty yards from them.

Pete said quietly in that sudden silence, "Go ahead, Blake. Only when you do it, hit the ground with a gun in your hand."

Blake, closest to the sheds, had his foot free of the stirrup, his weight forward. Now he settled back in the saddle again, and shuttled his baleful gaze to Mellish.

Ben didn't say anything, nor did he move. A meager smile started on his weathered face. "Well, well," he said softly.

Ed Briedehoff stepped out of the shack then, and stood just a little behind Pete. Ben noticed him and then looked at the house, as if expecting more.

"Just like a cuckoo clock, Ben," Ed drawled. "Start it off. Maybe there's some more inside."

Ben ignored this and swiveled his gaze down to Pete. "This is better than I thought," he said mildly. "Lots better." To Swan he said, "I've got a paper in my pocket you'd like to see," and he reached up to his shirt pocket and drew out a sheet of new paper, folded twice. He held it out to Swan, but Swan made no move to take it, nor did he show any curiosity.

"I'll read it, then," Ben said, still amiably.

He unfolded the paper and read, " 'Wanted, for murder of Frank Mellish on May the twenty-third, Pete Yard. Age, about twenty-eight; height, even six feet; weight—' " He looked at Swan. "You likely recognize him, Swan, since he's standin' right beside you." He paused and turned the paper face toward them. "Maybe those figures in heavy black at the top will interest you, Swan. It says five thousand dollars reward." He dropped the paper and folded his arms, and leaned on the saddle horn, smiling.

"You said somethin' awhile back," Swan said stubbornly. "If you ain't in the mind to now, kindly get the hell off this place."

Ben nodded and straightened up. "Sure. I'll be back tonight, though, Swan."

"I doubt that."

"Don't. I'll be back with Sheriff Nance. You better saddle up and ride, Swan, if you don't aim to be taken back to Ten Troughs."

Swan allowed himself a dour smile. "Even Nance can't jail a man for mindin' his own business."

Ben leaned forward and said, "But he can jail a man for hidin' an outlaw, Swan." He settled back in his saddle. "Tell your wife to pack up, too, Swan. Because I'll have my men in here by the time Nance is through with you. To Pete he said, "And you, Yard— We'll meet again." He saluted lazily and wheeled his horse. Swan's gun was halfway to his shoulder when Ed reached out and shoved the barrel down and let Swan curse in bitter impotence while the Anchor riders took the road and disappeared.

Ed was the first to move then. He walked over to the paper Mellish dropped and picked it up and read it, and then raised his eyes to Pete Yard.

"Did you know about this?"

Pete only shook his head. Ed dropped the note, saying gently, "It comes to me, Yard, that this is an easier way for Ben Mellish to get Swan than taking the place with his men."

Pete made a quick movement, and when it was completed Ed was looking into the cocked Colt held in Pete's square hand.

"You're a good man, Ed," Pete murmured. "A little too suspicious, but that never hurt a man." He circled a little to get Swan within easy range, but his eyes held no animosity, only a kind of wary pity. "Things come a little too fast for me here, but I'll get onto it," he said.

"If you live," Ed said. "There'll be a lot of us hunting you."

Pete nodded and said to Swan, "I didn't look for this, Swan. This is my fault."

Swan looked over at Ed. "Who is he?"

"Pete Yard, one of Mellish's understrappers. Ben sent him over to me, and I brought him to you, and now Ben has got you by the short hairs, Swan. He'll claim to Nance that he tried to take Yard away from us and we wouldn't give him up. Nance will come out and take you into custody and then Ben moves in."

Pete said, "Swan, you can't dodge it now. You throw in with Ed and Miles and whoever else you can get and hold this place tonight. Don't let Nance take you. If you do, your place is gone."

Ed said with bitter anger, "Swan is likely to call on me and Miles for help, ain't he, after I brought you up to him."

"Swan, drop that gun!" Pete said swiftly, and there was nothing in his voice now but business. Swan knew it, too, and he let the rifle slack from his hands, his face dark with anger. Pete said, "Now you, Ed."

When both rifles were on the ground, Pete kicked them

out of reach.

"Now call your wife, Swan. Tell her to bring the horses."

Swan did. Mrs. Ullman did not even see Pete's gun until she handed him the reins, and then she backed away from him, eyes wide.

Pete swung into the saddle, and then regarded the two men watching. "Everything I do won't be this sorry," he murmured. "You fight, that's all."

"And you run," Ed said curtly.

Pete expected a shot when he was out of pistol range, but neither Swan nor Ed made a move to pick up their rifles until he was out of sight. Pete took the same trail he had used coming over, but at Ed's place he struck off into the timber, riding hard. For an hour then, keeping to ridges free of brush, he cut down the slope into the open, and then reined up and looked back over the Basin. The road ribboned into sight at a dozen places, and through one of these far to the north he saw a band of riders, the dust funneling up behind, following them. That would be Ben Mellish, bound for town.

Pete put his horse down on the road and traveled at a fast walk and sometimes a trot through the long hours.

There was an expression of wry disgust on his face as he rode into the afternoon, feeling the wash of heat on his shoulders and the brooding loneliness of this country. The bright green of the new grass lay all about him, a solid, almost monotonous color against the depth of the bare sky. His first effort to help these ranchers had been turned against them, and in such a way that they thought he was a Mellish man. He didn't blame Ed, for his reasoning was inescapable. Restlessly Pete turned his mind to Nance, and tried to recall what Steve had said of him. Perhaps not dishonest, but prejudiced in favor of his nephew, Ben Mellish. That meant Nance, on hearing Ben's story of Swan refusing to turn over a wanted man, would come out and take Swan off his place. After a day and night of questioning, during which Swan would insist that he had not known Yard was outlawed, he would be freed, but the harm would have been done. Ben would have Swan's place, just as he had promised.

Pete swore quietly. Wherever he turned he seemed to bring misfortune with him. First it was to Christina Mellish, then to Ed, whom Swan would suspect, and to Swan.

At dusk, not far from Ten Troughs, Pete decided that this could not happen to Swan, and he felt better. But it was only at the sight of Ten Troughs lights shining aslant into the deep dust of the main street that he remembered he was a wanted man. It served to make him check his pony's pace for a moment, and then he went on.

Like a thousand of its sister towns, Ten Troughs had no graduations between town and country. Houses squatted on the cross street behind the main street, leaving the ragged line of stores to face the road, the last store being the town limits.

Pete pulled off the road and turned down the alley which ran behind the block of business houses and their sheds. In its friendly darkness he dismounted. The muted noises of the town drifted over to him from the street, making more deep and vast the solitude he had just left. This was a friendless town now, he was thinking, but it would not be hostile to him until later. He could walk its streets and not be recognized, save for two or three people, and they would not be likely to give him away. He smiled faintly in that dark, remembering Doctor Benbow, and then his face grew secretly troubled as he recalled Christina Mellish's face. But he put this thought aside and he stepped onto the boardwalk at the very end of it and made his slow way toward the center of town. *Sheriff Ross Nance, he thought with pleasure, has put five thousand dollars on the head of a man he will not recognize.*

But nevertheless, instinct warned him to be wary, even though Ben Mellish was a good half hour behind him. Crossing each barred island of light from the store windows he moved toward the center of town. At Pearson's Emporium he cut across the street to the far side. Only a few people were on the streets, for this was the Ten Troughs supper hour.

At the arch of the feed stable he paused and considered

the light in the office to the far side of it, then walked toward it and opened the door and entered. A young boy was looking over a saddle catalogue, his feet on the cold stove.

"Sheriff Nance have a horse here, bud?" he asked, and the boy nodded. Pete said, "Saddle him up, will you?" and left.

Across the street the high wide porch of the hotel relieved the solid stretch of store fronts. Beyond it, two doors down, was the office of the sheriff, which was not housed in the tiny courthouse up the cross street.

Pete went up street to the corner, crossed, and walked down past the sheriff's office, glancing in at the uncurtained window as he passed. Nance was in conversation with another man, who was leaning against the desk and listening with careful attention. Pete tramped on, and at the corner of the hotel porch, where the shadow was the deepest, he drew aside and leaned against the wood of its high frame. Two men came out of the hotel and down the steps and glanced at him, and Pete nodded and got an acknowledgment. A wagon jolted up from a side street and crossed to the other one, the slack knocking of its ungreased hubs waning with distance.

Pete shifted his flat shoulders and drew out a sack of tobacco and began to roll a smoke. Someone came down the steps and turned his way, but he did not look up until the footfalls ceased. When he did he saw Chris Mellish before him. The startled expression was still on her face.

"Pete!" she whispered and then looked about her. From the saddle shop next to the hotel a lone cowpuncher came out and turned their way.

Pete said quietly, "Talk up. Nobody knows me," and lighted his cigarette as the puncher passed.

"Why are you here?" Chris said swiftly. "Don't you know?"

Pete looked searchingly at her and let the match die. "I heard," he told her, unsmiling. "It was your brother I was supposed to kill—Chris."

"But you didn't! I know that. But you must think other

people know it!"

Pete laid a hand on her arm and said, "Easy. You and Doc are the only two people who know me here. There was no picture on that reward dodger."

Only then did the tension in Chris's face loosen, and the serene beauty of it was without trouble or fear. She smiled, and Pete could see the color begin to creep up into her face.

"Didn't Doc Benbow tell you what I said the morning I left?" Pete asked quietly.

"About my leaving?"

Pete nodded, and Chris said, "Yes. He told me. He—he even offered to send me south."

"It would save you a lot of heartbreak," Pete murmured. "I mean that. I meant it then—and I reckon I mean it even more now."

Chris said quickly, "Then you've seen Ben?"

"Yes."

"Have you—is he—"

"We haven't yet," Pete said. "I hope we never do. But somebody is going to nail up his hide, Chris, and it won't be nice to see."

Chris looked away for a moment. "I can face that. I think I already knew it before you ever told me."

"And you don't care?"

Chris's gaze met his. "He's my blood. You know I do," she said faintly. "But not enough to stop it. We pay for what we take or get, I think. We should, anyway."

"Do we?" Pete murmured, a little angry with her stubbornness. How could he tell her that Ben Mellish was not still a big and stubborn boy, that he was playing the deadliest of games, and one which, by any reckoning, he was bound to lose? It wasn't that she was innocent, and would be hurt by it, for she was a woman who had known trouble. Her face was tempered by it, shadowed and a little grave as he looked down into it now. But there was a high, clean pride there, too, that would bow and break under the news that Ben was a cheap hired bully with nothing to excuse him save an unnatural greed. She was watching

Pete's face now, asking silently for a strength he could not give her.

His eyes narrowed a little and he repeated, "Do we? I'm not sure. You held a gun on a man once, and because you did, I'm still alive. By my reckoning that's a debt. But I'm in this trouble up to my neck, and so is Ben. One of us will go down. If it's Ben that goes instead of me, and because of me, that will be a strange way to pay off my debt to you."

"Because of you?" Chris repeated.

Pete shifted impatiently. "When a man frames another, it's because he wants him out of the way. And I won't leave."

"And that's what I'm supposed to run from?" Chris asked, her voice a little angry, too. "Just because it has to be done and it might be you who does it?"

"He's your brother, Chris, whether he's right or wrong. You just said so."

"I know," she said quietly, suddenly humble.

Pete glanced down at the sheriff's office now. No one had come out. While he was looking, Chris said quietly, "There's a woman looking for you, Pete."

Pete's gaze whipped around to her face. "A woman? Who?"

"She won't tell her name." She was watching Pete's face, and the surprise in it was genuine, and Chris, strangely relieved, continued, making her voice as impersonal as she could. "She came to Sheriff Nance and asked about you. He sent her to Doctor Benbow, who wasn't in, and Mrs. Carew sent her to me." She raised her eyes now to the porch and nodded her head slightly. "There she is on the steps." Chris turned to go, but Pete laid a hand on her arm and looked over his shoulder. There, at the head of the porch steps, was Sylvia Waranrode; and Chris, her eyes steady on Pete's face, saw his lips pull tight and then form a soundless curse.

Sylvia came hurriedly down the steps, the rich cloth of her divided skirt swishing in her haste.

She said swiftly to Pete, "It's true, Pete! They are after

you! You've got to come with me!"

"I know," Pete said. He inclined his head toward Chris, whose arm he was squeezing hard. "Sylvia, this is my fiancée, Miss Mellish," he said quietly.

Before, Sylvia's darkly beautiful face had held a concern that Chris instinctively feared, understood, but now it changed slowly, and she saw the pride in this woman rally to hide something that Chris did not need to have named. And Chris felt a sudden hatred for Pete and his lie. She turned to him, mouth open to speak, trying to wrench free her arm, but he held it in an iron grip and in his eyes for one moment was a cool desperation, so that the words died on her lips.

"Oh," Sylvia said faintly. She gave one long look at Chris and inclined her head and said graciously, "She's been very kind to me, Pete." Sylvia looked down at her hands and then again at Pete, and she contrived an unreal smile. "I didn't know, Pete," she said huskily. "So—so much has happened since you left." She even laughed now. "I rather imagine my concern was for nothing, then."

Pete inclined his head slightly, keeping a tight hold on Chris's arm.

"Even the reward poster?" Sylvia asked slowly. "They are after you?"

"That's true," Pete said.

"Then—" Sylvia looked from Pete to Chris, and Chris could almost imagine that Sylvia was thinking Pete had dared to come into this town to keep a tryst with her.

"You go back to the hotel, Sylvia," Pete put in gently. "I'll have a man take you over to the reservation tomorrow."

Without a word Sylvia turned and ran up the steps and into the hotel, and Pete watched her with impassive eyes.

Chris said hotly, passionately, "That was cruel, terribly cruel!"

Pete didn't speak for a moment, and then he said grimly, "I'm sorry about that lie. But if you see somethin' in the path of a train, it doesn't matter whether you lead it away or kick it away, does it?" He added less irritably,

"She won't repeat it. I'm sorry I had to pull you in it, but you were closest."

"But it's not that!" Chris said swiftly. "She loves you! Are you so blind you don't see it?"

Pete did not hear this. He was looking down the street and he saw a man leaving the sheriff's office. He said to Chris, "If you'll tell Doc Benbow to send a man along with her—" And then his voice trailed off, for Sheriff Nance stepped out of the door and was locking it. Pete said quietly, "You'll have to go," and he left her, walking toward the sheriff's office.

When he came abreast Sheriff Nance he stopped. "Ben Mellish is outside town, Nance," he said. "He wants you." Gesturing toward the feed stable, he added, "I already told them to have your horse saddled."

Nance peered up at him. "Where's the trouble now?"

"Swan Ullman's."

"What is it?"

"Maybe you better let Ben tell you," Pete murmured. "I'll be waiting at the end of the street. And if no one sees you, Ben said it would be better."

Before Nance could question him further, Pete wheeled and started back toward his horse. He saw the sheriff cross to the feed stable.

It was a long minute Pete spent at the head of the street, listening for Mellish and his riders, watching for Nance. When Nance approached, Pete swung in beside him and pointed off to the right.

"This is mighty mysterious," Nance said. "Where is he?"

"Off toward the Ute."

They rode for fifteen or twenty minutes across country, saying nothing. Finally Nance said, "Are you sure about this?"

Pete said quietly, "If you look behind and to your right, Nance, you'll see you're bein' followed."

Nance twisted around in his saddle to look and Pete reached over and noiselessly drew Nance's single gun from its sheath at his hip.

"Followed?" Nance murmured. "Who by?"

Pete gently laid the nose of the gun in the small of Nance's back and drawled, "Your conscience."

CHAPTER TEN

STEVE WAS STANDING in the door of the line shack when Nance and Pete rode across the park to it next afternoon. He waved lazily at Pete, but he was looking at Nance, and a slow smile began to spread over his homely face.

"Ah, Sheriff." He greeted Nance gravely when they reined up before him. "So you've come 'way up here to serve your inciting-to-riot warrant. How does it read?"

Nance's grin was faint, unpleasant. None of this was to his liking, but he was a man who fully understood the situation without understanding his men and he wanted to go carefully. He nodded his head toward Pete. "Friend of yours?"

"The best."

"Then you're both in for it."

Steve looked over at Pete. "In for what, Pete?" he asked. He had already noticed that Nance was without his gun, while Pete had two of them rammed in his waistband. Pete swung off his horse and stretched.

"Nance claimed on a reward dodger that he wanted to see me about five thousand dollars' worth. I'm givin' him a look."

"You won't get away with it," Nance said gently.

Pete said idly, "I did, didn't I? You better light."

While they unsaddled, Pete told Steve of Ben Mellish's attempt to take over Swan Ullman's place. He talked as if Nance were not there, and the sheriff did not miss a word. Steve listened to it all and did not stop grinning.

Inside, the sheriff took one of the bunks while Steve built up the fire and Pete sliced steaks from a saddle of elk. Steve pointed to the elk and said, "That wasn't here when I left."

"Stumbling Bear came back."

Steve motioned with his head toward Nance, his glance questioning, and Pete said, "Why not? He'll know when we bust it."

"All right."

Pete laid his knife gently on the table and talked quietly. "The meeting of the chiefs was called to make talk about the dam, farming—and the sale of reservation lands."

"Did it pass?"

"It did," Pete said. "The chiefs didn't like it. Demarest —he's the agent from Washington—promised them plows and harness and houses and made them take it."

"What lands are up for sale?" Steve asked.

Pete smiled narrowly. "Before I tell you that, tell me where you went and what you learned."

Steve slapped the steaks in the fry-pan and then squatted against the wall. Wherever he had been he had picked up the clothes of cattleland—Levi's, worn boots, even a gun which he wore self-consciously strapped to a hip.

"First I went over to that little jerk-line teamsters' stop of Bend," Steve said. "You know it? A general store and a feed corral and a house and five sheds. It's the county seat of Waranrode County."

"I know it. Why did you go there?"

"To try and find out exactly where Waranrode's range was. I thought maybe a piece of it would border on the Ute reservation."

"It doesn't."

"That's what the storekeeper told me," Steve said. "I pretended I wanted to lease range, so he blocked out for me on the map all the outfits bordering the Ute reservation. I began to work on the ones on the north line."

"How?"

"I'd ride in to each spread and tell them I wanted to run cattle in this country and since all the land was taken I wanted to lease some of theirs." He grinned up at Pete. "Isn't that the way it's done?"

Pete nodded and asked, "What did you find out?"

"That they'd all lease me land except one outfit, the Schumacher brothers. They wouldn't lease for any price. They wouldn't sell for three times what the place was worth. They wouldn't talk, either. You know them?"

Pete nodded, attentive.

"Then I accused them of not even owning the place. I got run off then. I don't think they do own it, but I can't prove it because all the county records are with Waranrode." He smiled again. "So, being suspicious, I figured that Waranrode owned the Schumachers."

"That's a guess," Pete said quickly.

"Wait till I finish. Schumachers' range is on the north boundary of the reservation. The east boundary is the Walking River badlands. I didn't know anything about the south boundary—the spreads on it—but I wanted to do a thorough job. I rode south and inquired from the few spreads on the south boundary about leased land. They were willing to lease—all except one."

"Whose?" Pete said slowly.

"Jim Lassiter, who owns the Chevron on the edge of the Lowenweep Breaks. He's a leathery old boy with a big sandy mustache that covers half his face, so I couldn't see how he took it. He was almost polite. He wouldn't sell or lease. I went into Wheeler, the county seat of Humboldt County, and looked up his place. It belongs to him, all right."

Pete's face lost some of its tension, settling into its usual, hard indolence. Nance, who had been listening attentively all this while, shifted in his seat and said nothing.

Steve was smiling, watching Pete. "But I asked questions," Steve murmured. "I found out things. Things like this—that Lassiter doesn't ship fifty head of stock a year, that he pays his bills yearly and in a lump sum, that he hasn't any friends there and doesn't drink or talk. What does that prove to you?"

Pete didn't answer. He was watching Steve closely.

Steve answered his own question. "It proves that Lassiter has that place registered in his own name, but he's running it for somebody else. Like the Schumacher brothers, only more so. So Waranrode could own the Schu-machers' place and the Chevron."

"And if he did?" Pete murmured.

"It would prove that he aims to own that slice of reserva-tion between the two. And that slice, accordin' to the storekeeper's map, would stretch from the river to the Ute Lakes on the north, from a straight line south where you come to the edge of Lassiter's range. It runs on into the Lowenweep Breaks and Walking River." He paused, watching Pete. "What land did Stumbling Bear say was going up for sale?"

Pete said quietly, "The slice you just named."

Slowly Steve came to his feet. "Well, now," he drawled in a voice almost trembling, "who's suspicious now?"

Nance said, "Them steaks are burning."

Steve turned to rescue the steaks. Pete shuffled the plates out on the table, and without a word the meal was served up. Steve watched Pete, who sat down now, offered the plate of steaks to Nance, then settled back in his chair. Nance was watching Pete, too. He didn't understand all of this, but it was beginning to make sense.

Pete said quietly, frowning at his plate, "The Schu-machers and Lassiter would be the only logical bidders for that range at public sale. And Waranrode could buy it through them."

"Which is what he's planning to do," Steve said flatly.

Pete's gaze shuttled up to meet Steve's. "How would Waranrode be so sure this slice was goin' to be sold that he could buy both those places before the meeting of the chiefs? He was sure. And only one man could tell him. That's Linkman, the agent."

"You believe it, then, that this is what Waranrode is workin' for?"

Pete only nodded and began to eat. Presently Steve said, "The reason he started that Basin war was for a blind, then?"

"To get you in it," Pete said grimly. "And once in it, it'll be easy to kill you and shove the blame on a range war."

Nance looked swiftly at Pete, but he did not immediately say anything. Finally, he asked Pete, "What's Waranrode got to do with this Ten Troughs war?"

Pete said casually around a mouthful of elk meat, "Why, Nance, he's the man behind Big Ben Mellish. He's payin' him to grab that land." He pointed a fork at Steve. "For five years Steve Trueblood's newspaper has been the only one in the state that has fought Waranrode. Waranrode knew that sooner or later Steve would turn up this reservation fraud. So he paid Ben Mellish to start this fight in Ten Troughs, knowin' Steve would wonder how Ben Mellish got the information from Washington that a dam would be built. He knew Steve would get in the fight, just like he's done. And once in it, Steve would be killed. And once Steve was out of the way, nobody in this state has the guts to stand on their hind legs and call Waranrode a crook." Pete's eyes were scornful now. "Paste that in your hat, Nance, whether you believe it or not, and see who's right in the end."

Nance, his seamed face flushed an angry red, said nothing. He settled back to his eating and finished, then packed his pipe. Pete was already finished and had rolled his smoke. He was looking out the window, face somber. Nance glanced covertly at him, and suddenly it came to him that he listened to this recital with a rapt interest almost implying belief, and he was immediately angry with himself for showing this attention. To his stubborn and close way of thinking it showed a weakness in him, a lack of fight. So, after he lighted his pipe he said gently to Pete, "Why did you kill Frank Mellish, Yard?"

Pete lazily removed his gaze from the window, and in shuttling it to Nance he rested it for one brief second on Steve, who saw the light of warning.

Pete now regarded Nance with frowning attention. "Would it help you to know? I wouldn't tell this to a man I thought would turn it against me."

Nance flushed. "I'll turn it against you, Yard. That's my promise."

Pete shook his head gravely. "I'll have to see you don't."

"Why did you?" Nance insisted.

"Maybe you didn't understand," Pete murmured, quiet menace in his voice. "To put it simply, dead men don't talk." He paused meaningly. "You still want to hear it?"

Nance glared at him. If he backed down now it would seem to these two that he was afraid of them, which was, in all truth, contrary to fact. He said stubbornly, "I don't think you'd shoot a man in the back. And I want to know."

"All right, you asked for it," Pete said gravely. He looked out the window, as if assembling the facts of his story. He began with caution. "You remember when it was Frank Mellish was away from the Anchor for several months?"

"The last time?" Nance asked.

"No. Next to last."

Nance frowned. "Yes. Last year. He was gone for three months. Went over into Wyoming lookin' for breeding stuff."

That was all Pete needed. He turned to face Nance now. "That's what he said. But he never saw Wyoming, Nance. He sent a man on into Wyoming, but he never got farther himself than a little way station on the transcontinental."

"No?" Nance said curiously.

"No. And I'll tell you how I know it. I was workin' for Waranrode when I got a bad fall from a horse. Broke my hip. As soon as it started to mend I could walk around, but I couldn't ride. I wasn't any use to any outfit. I hadn't been home close onto ten years, and when Waranrode heard my folks lived just down in Toolle County he sent me home on a buckboard for a visit."

"That was pretty white for him," Steve murmured dryly.

Pete inclined his head. "We're a large family, us Yards— six girls and no other boys except me. It kept my dad hustling to provide for us, but he did. But only two of the girls are married, and it meant that some of them had to work to help out."

Steve was watching Pete now with alert skepticism. Pete

was talking to him more than to Nance, who was listening closely.

"One sister, Sue, worked at a restaurant in this little way station of Warms. Ever hear of it?" Both Steve and Nance shook their heads.

"Well, Frank Mellish got off the train there for a bite to eat. He saw Sue, and she's a beauty. I reckon Frank thought he could catch a later train. He wanted to sit there and look at her. Frank wasn't hard to look at, either, was he, Nance?"

Nance said, "A nice-lookin' boy."

"Sue thought so, too," Pete said quietly. "She took a likin' to him and brought him home to meet Dad and the family. We all liked him, right enough. He just stayed on at Warms to be around Sue until she quit her job, ready to marry him. They come back to the spread."

Pete looked gravely at Steve. "This next ain't very nice," he said soberly. To Nance he said, "He was your nephew, Nance. You want to hear it?"

"I do."

"All right. But you'll have to get a picture of our place in your mind. The house is big, made of stone, and it sprawls out like the old Mexican places. There was my six sisters, Dad, me, Frank, and four hands at the ranch. The place was big enough, so we all had separate rooms. Well, it was one night that my hip was troublin' me considerably and I couldn't sleep. I was lying there awake in the dark when I heard a noise. It was like somethin' bein' dropped and it came from the next room, where my sister, Emily, was sleepin'. I half-raised up to listen. I must have laid that way for two minutes. And then come an awful scream. I jumped out of bed and hobbled into Emily's room." He paused, his sober stare concentrated on Steve. "When I struck a light I saw Emily lyin' there, hands up to her face—and they was covered with blood."

Steve murmured curiously, "Was she killed?"

Pete shook his head grimly and looked hard at Steve. "Not killed. Worse, I reckon, for a girl, for her face had been spoiled. Somebody had crept into her room, slugged her into unconsciousness, and disfigured her."

"How?"

Pete touched the bridge of his nose. "A knife. They started right at the bridge of her nose and ripped right down with a knife. There was nothin' there, where her nose had been."

Steve, not looking at Nance, stared sharply at Pete, whose face was expressionless. Pete went on. "We never knew who did it. Dad had been havin' trouble with Utes over some lease land. Those southern Utes are bad, all of 'em, and he went over to the reservation and threatened the whole tribe with torture and death if he ever found out the man that did it."

Steve thought he understood now. He said, "This wasn't the sister Frank Mellish was goin' to marry?"

Pete shook his head gravely. "No. Not that time."

"You mean it happened again?" Steve asked softly. He looked amazed, shifting his gaze to Nance. Nance was edged forward on his chair a little, watching Pete with the closest attention.

"Again," Pete said. "The very next week. The girls doubled up after that, but Sue, she used to sit up late with Frank, and that left her the odd one when it came time to go to bed." He said softly, "A week later the same thing happened to her—same thing, same way." Without a pause he went on more quietly, "Frank was heartbroke, but he still wanted to marry her. Sue wouldn't see him. She kept in her room. Me and Dad spent every wakin' hour tryin' to find a clue left by the man who did it. We couldn't. He'd prised open a window in Sue's room the second time."

"What about the Utes?" Steve said in disgust.

"We had no proof," Pete continued grimly. "But this time I swore I'd do somethin'. We pulled two beds into the biggest room and Mary, Laura, Lillian, and Amelia slept there, and I put a blanket on the floor and slept beside them."

"And it stopped?" Steve asked.

"It did not," Pete continued in a husky, strained voice.

"Like I said, my hip wouldn't let me sleep much, itching the way it was with the break healin'. But I'd lay there awake and breathe regular, so the girls thought I slept. Well, one night a week and a half after that, I was lyin' there and I heard the window start to open out. I was where I couldn't see it, and I didn't dare move or I'd scare whoever it was. I laid there until I heard his boot drag acrost the floor, and then I sat up, strikin' a match with one hand and pointin' my gun with the other. I had him!"

"A Ute?" Steve said swiftly.

Pete said, "Frank Mellish."

Pete watched only Steve, whose face reflected amazement and disgust. "Frank Mellish?" Steve echoed softly. "You mean he'd—he'd done that to the woman he was goin' to marry?"

Pete only nodded.

"But why?" Nance asked curiously.

Pete said, "Let me go on. Frank threw up his hands, for he saw I had him. The girls wakened then and I made them be quiet. Then I walked over and hit him." Pete looked ashamed now, his face coloring a little. "I reckon I was so mad I was crazy. Then I searched him for a gun. I found somethin' in his pocket, wrapped up in a handkerchief, that made me go wild then. I'd of shot him if it hadn't been for Lillian puttin' her hand over the hammer of the gun."

"Found somethin'?" Steve echoed.

"What?" Nance demanded.

"Those—" Pete faltered. "Hell! It was what he had cut off from Emily's and Sue's faces. They was wrapped up in a bloody handkerchief, like a civilized Indian might carry scalps."

For a long while there was silence. Finally, Nance leaned forward and touched Pete's arm. "Did Frank say anything? Explain it?"

Pete, for the first time, looked at Nance. "He did," he said grimly. "When I asked Frank if he was crazy, he said this. These are his exact words, Nance. 'Pete, I got a legal excuse. Next year I'm runnin' for sheriff of Ten Troughs

County, and everybody knows that sheriff sticks his nose into everybody's business so much that I figured I'd need at least three more noses.' That's what he said."

Nance's face, for a moment, did not change, and then Steve let out a whoop of joy; and Nance sank back onto his seat, his face brick-red and sheepish and angry and marked with an agony of embarrassment. Pete laughed silently, his whole lean, flat body shaking with mirth.

Steve bawled with delight until he leaned against the wall and wiped tears from his eyes. Nance, face averted, was slowly rubbing the bowl of his pipe, and now he reached up, laid it on the table, and looked up at Pete. Across his seamed, usually grim face was a broad smile, and his chuckle was deep and amused.

He said gently, "Gentlemen, we'll call that killing solved. Only, I'm damned if I'm not the one that is dead."

When Steve had enough control of himself to sit down and smoke, he said to Pete, "What will we do with him? He should be in a crib, but we haven't one."

The sheriff grinned again.

"We can't leave him here," Steve said.

"If you got a rattle or some mud pies, I reckon I'd make out all right," Sheriff Nance said humbly.

"You'd run," Steve said a little sadly.

Nance nodded. "I would that."

"We could take your horse," Steve told him.

"I'd walk."

"We could take your boots."

"I'd tear up my coat for boots and still walk."

Pete grinned. Behind the officious bullheadedness of Nance was a humanness that Pete's riding and Steve's jibes were bringing out. Another time, in another situation, perhaps Nance would not have acted as he had done, Pete was thinking, when Steve said, "You want a jail, like you give your own prisoners. Is that it?"

Nance said, "If you can find it."

"I think I can," Steve murmured, looking over at Pete. "Bring the blankets and some grub and we'll saddle up."

The three of them, Nance in the middle, cut off back of

the shack down the slope and to the south. They traveled for a half hour when Steve reined up and pointed. Below them, just off the floor of a canyon on a small bench hewn of the rock of the canyon wall was a scattering of weathered tumbledown sheds around a shack.

Nance looked over at Steve. "I was afraid of that. I hoped you hadn't run into it."

Pete eyed Steve questioningly, but Steve pushed his horse down the slope and reined up before one of the sheds. He said to Nance, "Does the shaft go into the side of the hill or down?"

"It goes down."

Steve grinned and swung off his horse and walked around to the rear of the shack. A wide hole, fringed raggedly with weeds and overlaid with sawed slabs, was visible. Steve yanked the boards away and peered into it.

"Go down and try it," he said to Nance. "After all, you're the one to be satisfied."

The ladder was missing. Pete tied their three ropes together, and Nance, his foot in the loop of one, was lowered down the shaft. Only a little more than one lariat was played out before it slacked off. Steve leaned over and called to Nance, "Like it?"

"It's dry," Nance answered.

"Drafty?"

"No. They quit down here about thirty-forty feet."

Steve said, "I forgot to tell you, Nance. If you give your word not to make a break for it, you're welcome to the shack."

"I'll stay here," Nance said quietly.

Steve pulled up the rope and lowered the blankets and food and a canteen of water to Nance while Pete hobbled the sheriff's horse and turned him loose to graze.

Steve joined Pete, who was mounted and waiting. Steve swung into his saddle and said, "How long a ride is it to the reservation?"

"Fifteen miles." Pete glanced obliquely at Steve and then looked away, saying, "Reckon you could do this job?"

"Make Linkman talk?"

"Yes. Or whatever it is we've got to make him do."

"And we've got to," Steve murmured grimly. "He will talk, I think. How can he explain away the fact that Waranrode bought those two outfits before the Utes even decided on what piece of land to dispose of? No, he'll talk. If not to us, then an army committee." He was quiet a moment. "If he doesn't we're licked, Pete. Because, in a court, we'll never prove Mellish's connection with Waranrode. Linkman is the key. We'll make him talk some way."

"Reckon you could do it—alone?" Pete murmured.

Steve looked swiftly at him. "Alone? While you do what?"

"There's still men in the Ten Troughs Basin," Pete said thinly. "I'm not convinced yet they won't fight."

"That Basin isn't important," Steve said casually. "When we crush Waranrode, as we will when Linkman gives it away, we'll crush Mellish, too."

"But too late," Pete said mildly. "I'd hate that. You go over to the reservation. I'll head for Ten Troughs."

"You're wanted there."

"I know. What of it?"

Steve shifted faintly in his saddle and said gently, "You're a stubborn man, Pete. At the beginning I felt the way you do about those Basin ranchers. But they won't help themselves. We have to help them, and the real way is to strike at the roots of it—Waranrode—through Linkman."

"They'll fight," Pete said quietly.

Steve laughed now and turned his homely face to Pete. "Linkman can wait, eh?"

"Why not?"

"All right. Let's head for Ten Troughs." When Pete looked at him, a question in his eyes, Steve said quietly, "Two of us can work any game better than one. I'll stick with you."

CHAPTER ELEVEN

IT TOOK BEN MELLISH the better part of twenty minutes to become suspicious. Not finding Nance in his office and seeing the door was locked, Ben sent one of his men up to Nance's house, while he and his men went into the Melodian for a drink. The rider returned with the news that Nance hadn't been home for supper. Ben sent him out to find Jim Bonal, the part-time deputy. In ten minutes the rider was back at the Melodian.

"Jim said he left Nance at the office. He saw Nance come out and lock up and start off to supper."

"But he didn't!" Ben said impatiently.

The rider shrugged.

"Go over to the Exchange House dining-room and see if he's in there."

The rider returned to say he wasn't. Ben angrily pushed aside the bottle of whisky at his elbow. He looked around at all the games in progress and then said to the bartender, "Anyone in the back rooms, Harge?"

The bartender said no. Ben tramped out to the street and glared up and down it. The only time he really wanted and needed Nance, he couldn't be found. And then Ben remembered the feed stable, and turned down street to it.

He found the boy in the office. "Seen Sheriff Nance, son?"

"Sure. I give him his horse."

"When was that?"

The boy told him, adding, "A puncher come in and asked me was this the place Nance kept his horse. I said sure, and he said to saddle Nance's horse. I did it and then stood out in the stable for close to fifteen minutes watchin' him across the street, and then—"

"Watchin' who?"

"The puncher. He was waitin' for Nance."

"Didn't he go in the office?"

"No. He just waited by the hotel talkin' to people."

Ben, who had had his hand on the doorknob, now closed the door gently and said, "What did this puncher look like?"

"Tall, not so big as you, with a—"

"Was his face marked like he'd been in a fight?"

"That's him. Sure."

Ben said ominously, "You say he was talkin' to people. Who?"

The boy grinned. "That's what I was comin' to. He talked to your sister a long time and then another woman come down and he talked to them both for a minute. Then this other woman left and come over here and got her horse and rode off."

Ben wheeled and wrenched the door open, and then he paused and said, "Did you see the brand of the horse this woman was ridin'?"

"Sure. A new brand to me. G.W."

Ben crossed to the hotel and from the clerk found that Chris was in her room. He mounted the stairs two at a time. He found Chris's room door open and walked inside. Doc Benbow sat in the lone armchair and Chris, pillows at her back, was sitting on the bed. There was a faint sweetish smell of whisky in the room.

Ben, breathing hard, glared at Chris and said bluntly, "Get out of here, Doc."

Chris looked at Doc Benbow. "Stay, please."

Ben shut the door behind him and came over to the foot of the bed and placed both fisted hands on its footboard. "I just learned Pete Yard was in town," he said thickly.

"Did you?"

"I heard you talked to him."

"I did," Chris said quietly.

Ben, for once, was almost speechless with anger. Doc was smiling a little, watching Chris.

"The man who killed your brother," Ben said angrily.

"The man—"

"What is it you want, Ben?" Chris cut in coldly.

Ben leaned forward a little. "Why, your friend, Pete Yard, has just kidnaped the sheriff, that's all," he said sardonically. "Since you seem to be the single friend that tramp has got in this town, I thought he might have told you where he took him."

"He didn't," Chris said, "but I'm glad he took him."

Ben straightened a little and unfisted his hands to clasp the footboard, his high and burly body throwing a gargantuan shadow against the far wall.

"You are?" he said softly.

"Yes. You've bullied Uncle Ross into a place where that's probably the only thing that will keep him from getting killed!"

Ben smiled wickedly. "So he's had you, too—like that other slut he talked to tonight. He—"

Doc Benbow's low-pitched voice cut into Ben's wrath and stopped it. "Ben," Doc said, "you're a damned, foulmouthed scoundrel! Get out of here before I let this thing off at your back!"

Ben turned slowly to confront Doc, who had not risen from his chair. In Doc's hand was a new, shining six-gun, and behind the contempt Ben could see in his eyes was a baleful warning.

Ben laughed, looking over at Chris, whose face was taut and pale. There was a magnificent scorn in his face as he said, "Drunks and murderers. That's prime company for a wench like you, Sis."

Doc let the gun off then, and its blast filled the room in a prolonged crash. As its echo died there was a faint sifting of plaster to the floor from a hole in the far wall.

Ben only laughed and turned his back to Doc and walked out the door, closing it after him.

Doc was on his feet, cocking the stiff-springed gun with both hands, and over his face was a fury that made Chris leap to her feet and run to him.

"Uncle Doc! Don't! Don't!" She laid a hand on his arm.

Doc looked up then, his eyes fogged over, and then he

let his gun hand drop. He sighed gustily and looked at the floor.

"He had a good mother," Doc said huskily, "but he's a bastard to every decent thing she taught him. I meant to kill him."

Chris led him to his chair and gently forced him to sit down. He sat there a long moment, letting the color wash out of his face; and he passed a hand over his eyes and looked up at Chris. "It's not the drunk part, I don't mind that." He smiled a little now. "But I guess I haven't the humanity to remember a man is insane who calls you that, Chris."

Chris smiled wanly and sat down on the bed.

"You've got to get out of here," Doc said, and Chris nodded absently. Doc rose and came over to stand in front of her. "I know you don't want to leave. You think that would be running away, and for you, maybe that's right. I reckon it is. But you've got to get away from Ben until this thing is settled one way or the other." He waited a moment. "Do you know a place you can go?"

"I'll visit someone tomorrow, Uncle Doc," Chris said. "Now, would you mind leaving?"

Doc walked over and picked up his hat from the washstand. "It strikes me," he said without looking at Chris, "that our friend Pete is a man who knows how to crowd his luck."

Chris only looked at him, and Doc put on his hat. He was his old self now, his eyes humorous and skeptical and his voice dry, gentle. He walked past her and patted her shoulder and paused. "It also strikes me that you should reserve your verdict until all the facts are in."

Chris looked up at him swiftly. "What do you mean, Uncle Doc?"

"Something happened before I came up."

Chris flushed a little. "What?"

"Damned if I know," Doc murmured. "You do. Good night, honey."

Doc let himself out and headed with the instinct of a homing pigeon for the bar of the Melodian.

Chris sat just as Doc had left her, thinking over his last words. Without being told the whole story, he knew something had happened, and in his wise and gentle way was trying to advise her without violating her privacy. And thinking this, Chris blushed, and was immediately angry with herself. She had told Doc of Pete's coming into town, as if there were no price on his head, as if he didn't care even if there was. When she came to the part about Sylvia she had told it to Doc without a change of voice, but she did not mention Pete's claiming her as his fiancée, nor did she mention Sylvia's beautiful face. Doc had watched her keenly, smiling a little, so that she remembered evading his eyes. And now she wondered why she had had to make an effort to be casual with Doc. What was there about Pete Yard's knowing a woman who loved him that should upset her? For Chris knew this Sylvia loved Pete, and she was a woman of breeding and beauty and intelligence and loyalty, all those things that a man looks for in a woman. And Pete had been brutal to her, had lied to her, but in a way that made Chris think he had done it to save her from something. She tried to remember Pete's face when he first saw Sylvia. There was surprise and a quick stirring of anger before his face settled into that rather hard, indolent indifference that was his usual expression; nothing about it indicated that he loved this woman.

Chris sprang up with sudden anger, and furiously started to undress. Why had she let herself think of these things, as if any of it mattered or could influence her empty way of life?

Next morning she got her horse and rode out south. It had been many months since she had visited or seen Mrs. Wells, and she knew she would be welcome. The Wellses lived on the western edge of the reservation, and Chris rode up to their place in midafternoon and was welcomed with a kiss and a giant hug by Mrs. Wells, who had followed Dave Mellish and his bride into this country.

Mrs. Wells was a robust, openhearted woman, whose two sons and husband were riding that afternoon. Normal-

ly she was a cheerful soul who loved the gossip she so
sorely missed; but this afternoon, as Chris helped her in
the kitchen of the two-story log house that looked out
beneath a tangle of trees to the sun-baked, mesa-shot reservation lands, Mrs. Wells carefully avoided any mention of
Ben or Frank, except to say that they had not heard of
Frank's death until too late to attend the funeral. Chris
murmured something in embarrassment, but there was
nothing more to say, and she understood as well as Mrs.
Wells that the loyalty of Anchor neighbors was a thing of
the past; that it was a thing of which no one would gladly
talk.

That evening, around the huge supper table, spare,
lean Hod Wells was the same way. They talked of town,
of cattle, of the dam, of fall market prospects, of the Indians, of the weather, of a thousand things, but never of
Ben Mellish and the fortunes of the Anchor. Afterward,
toward bedtime, when the brooding starlit lands about
them seemed to hush them all to silence as they sat clustered on the long dark porch, Chris was grateful. If this
acting had continued another hour, she could not have
stood it.

And in the clean, spartan bedroom she lay sleepless,
letting all this recent history march in ordered bitterness
through her tired memory. And, inevitably, it settled on
Pete Yard, this obscure and lonely man who was fighting
no battle of his own. Tonight, with nothing that was
familiar around her, Chris let herself think of him. But
it was shared, for the image of Sylvia, whose last name she
never heard and never wanted to hear, rose up to stand
beside Pete. Chris made up a romance about them, and
hated herself for doing it. She thought of those hard and
brutal words Pete had said to Sylvia, and again she pitied
this woman. It seemed needlessly cruel of Pete to take
the arm of a strange woman and say to Sylvia, "This is the
woman I am going to marry." And why? Because he
wanted to get her away from Ten Troughs—and for a
reason Chris did not understand.

With startling abruptness it occurred to Chris that

Sylvia no longer needed to believe that lie, for she had left Ten Troughs. And with a measure of peace of mind Chris slept then.

Next morning she saddled her horse alongside Hod Wells. She had pleaded the excuse that she had to return to town. But once free of the place she swung in a wide circle to the south, and by noon was deep in the reservation lands.

A little before dark she rode into the post. It lay scattered on a grassy shoulder of land free of trees and bare as a table top except for the slim willows which hid the shallow banks of narrow Ute River below it.

A rough wagon road formed the only street, and in ragged disarray on either side of it were the skin and canvas tepees of the Utes. A hundred dogs skulked about the camp and only a few of them bothered to come up and harry her pony with their barking. Wide-eyed children dressed in a laughable mixture of ill-fitting store clothes and buckskin watched her and did not speak. Campfires burned in front of many of the tepees, the smoke hanging in a gray blanket in the evening air. Dotting this army of tepees were a few log cabins, ill-constructed, roofed with brush, doorless, yards littered with offal. Pole corrals stood cheek by jowl with tepees and shacks, and through it all moved a straight spiritless people who seemed never to have a word for each other.

At the far end of the post a long stone building announced the quarters of a white trader. Behind it were the stone foundations of the old army barracks long since burned. And set back from the road, past the trading-post, were the neat grounds of the agent and its two-story, sawed-board house with a corner porch jutted up far higher than the new trees and shrubs planted within the white-painted picket fence. Behind it a barn and corral were placed in neat regularity.

Chris dismounted at the gate with some misgivings. She had only heard Pete tell Sylvia to go to the reservation; and now that she was here, she was beginning to wonder if her trip had been for nothing.

Opening the gate, Chris noticed in the dusk that the fence swung in to meet one corner of the house, and that in front of the fence were tie rails. A bright light shone from the two windows of this corner, and she guessed this must be the office of the Indian agent.

At the door her knock was answered by a fat Ute servant.

"Is—is Sylvia in?" Chris asked.

The Indian only gazed at her blankly. Chris could see into the house, and its large living-room was glowing with dim lamps.

"Is Sylvia in?" Chris asked. "A dark girl—"

Suddenly Sylvia Waranrode appeared at the side of the servant, who vanished noiselessly.

Sylvia looked at Chris and immediately recognized her and smiled.

"Oh, Miss Mellish. Come in." Sylvia held the door wide.

Chris stepped into the room. "I didn't know who to ask for," she said a little shyly. "You see, I never heard your last name."

Sylvia was dressed in the same dark-green riding-suit she had been wearing in Ten Troughs. She closed the door just as an older woman entered the room from another doorway. She was a heavy woman with a stupidly amiable face, and Sylvia said to her, "Mrs. Linkman, this is Christina Mellish, the girl whom I was to meet here."

Chris looked swiftly at Sylvia and then shook hands with Mrs. Linkman, the wife of the agent. "You're welcome, my dear. You're riding late and must be hungry. Sylvia, show her to your room to tidy up. Supper's only a minute away. You'll stay the night, of course, Miss Mellish."

Sylvia took Chris's arm and led her into a bedroom, escaping the torrential stream of Mrs. Linkman's aimless chatter. Sylvia shut the door behind her and leaned on it, smiling a little.

"I'm getting quite expert at lying," she said, "as you've probably noticed. But you must stay somewhere tonight."

Chris took off her gloves and sat down on the bed.

"I—I shouldn't have come here," she said, with hesitation, looking at Sylvia. "But there was something I had to tell you."

Sylvia said, her voice toneless, "About Pete?"

"Yes. You see, he lied to you that night about me—about us. We are not engaged. We scarcely know each other."

Sylvia felt something stir deep within her, something close to hope. She said evenly, "I'm afraid I don't understand."

"I was afraid you wouldn't," Chris said gently. "You see, I was earning money at Doctor Benbow's in Ten Troughs as a nurse for Pete. He was there five days. We didn't speak a hundred words, perhaps, and I didn't know his name until later—much later."

Sylvia crossed the room to stand in front of Chris. She looked down at this woman whom she had been hating for two days now, and looked searchingly at her clean, troubled face.

"Then why did Pete do it?" Sylvia asked.

"I don't know. I asked him—after you left—for I was shamed by him, and by you. He only apologized and said, 'If you see someone in the path of a train, it doesn't matter much whether you lead them away or kick them away.' Then he left."

Sylvia didn't answer for a moment. She said next, "What did he mean?"

"I don't even know that. I thought perhaps you might understand it."

"And you came clear over here to tell me that—just that?" Sylvia asked gently.

"Yes, I thought you should know."

"Why?"

Chris looked deep into her eyes. "Because he hurt you."

"Nothing else?" Sylvia murmured.

"Yes. Because you love him."

Without hesitation Sylvia nodded. Turning, she walked over to the dresser and faced it, her back to Chris.

"I'm sorry," Chris said. "It was cruel of him—and I don't

think he meant it when he said it."

Slowly Sylvia turned around to face Chris. For a moment she didn't comment and then she smiled faintly. "My dear, that was kind of you. But it is unfeminine."

"I—I don't understand."

"I think you do. It is unfeminine—because you love him, too."

Chris came to her feet, her hands clenched tightly, her face pale, eyes staring at Sylvia. "Why do you say that?" she asked swiftly.

"How did you know I loved him?" Sylvia countered.

"It's—it's something you can't hide. I could see it in your face."

"And I can see it in yours." She came across the room and took Chris's hands, then tilted Chris's chin up so that she could see into her eyes. "Are you ashamed of it? I am proud of it."

Chris held herself tensely for a second, then a deep sob racked her, and Sylvia gathered her into her arms. Chris cried brokenly while Sylvia said nothing, and then, as suddenly, she tried to stifle her tears.

"It's true," Chris murmured. "I'm not ashamed of it. Only I didn't want to. I wouldn't let myself think it."

Sylvia moved her over to the bed and sat down beside her, and while Chris smothered her sobbing Sylvia talked in a low voice.

"If she is lucky, once in a lifetime a woman will love a man like him. He's not good. He's been drunk in a thousand towns and he loves to fight and he has known other women and he has stolen when he was hungry, and if he had done none of these things I don't think I would love him so much. But he is kind and gentle and strong, and he can walk alone. But he is too proud to do that. I have seen men who love him and who take some of his fairness and gentleness and strength for their own when they have been with him. If I were a man and he was my friend I would die for him. And if I were a woman—any woman— I could not help loving him."

Chris listened. "I do not know him well, but I know all

that is true."

"I do know him well," Sylvia murmured. "For three years he has taken me a hundred miles to put me on a train for school in the East. And for three years I have thought I would die if I couldn't see him. And each time he met me again he was the same. He was wise and tolerant, but he was hard with me, too. And he never loved me."

Chris said, "Are you sure?"

Sylvia laughed bitterly. "Can a woman ever mistake that? Yes, I am sure." She looked at Chris. "But it will make no difference. I want him, and I will fight for him."

Chris said quietly, "So will I."

"I know. And I think you are better armed than I am," Sylvia murmured.

"Armed?"

"Yes. You have his gentleness, and no one can fight that."

"But so have—"

The sharp, flat, racketing roar of a gunshot hammered through the house, bringing Chris and Sylvia to their feet. They looked at each other, then Sylvia ran for the door.

Mrs. Linkman was standing in the corridor, her mouth sagging, eyes round.

"What is it?" Sylvia demanded.

"The office," Mrs. Linkman answered hysterically.

Sylvia ran down the corridor, Chris behind her, Mrs. Linkman behind her.

Sylvia swung the door open and immediately stopped, a sharp, horrified cry escaping her lips. Then she walked in, and Chris saw it, too.

Sprawled across the floor of the tiny lamplit office, face down, was the figure of a sandy-haired man in the uniform of army blue. His arms were flung out over his head, and his cheek rested in a tiny pool of blood.

"Major Linkman!" Sylvia breathed, and then turned to Mrs. Linkman, who just entered the room. Her shriek echoed through the house and then Sylvia was by her side.

"Get help!" Sylvia commanded Chris. "I'll see to her."

Sylvia put her arms around Mrs. Linkman and led her out of the office, leaving Chris alone with the dead man. Chris's eye traveled from the body to an object lying in the middle of the floor. It was a glove, huge in size, even at this distance. Chris skirted the body and kneeled by it, and she felt a sudden nausea rise within her. It was Ben Mellish's glove, and though she had not seen him wearing this very one with the hole cut out of the palm, she had noticed the new pair he wore that night in her hotel room, and it, too, had had the palm cut from it, to ease his blistered hand.

Blindly she picked it up and thrust it into the bosom of her dress and then ran through the outside door into the night.

She heard the pounding of approaching feet, and then a voice asked her, "Was that a shot?"

"Yes. Inside." Chris followed the man in. Evidently it was the trader, the only other white man besides the doctor on the reservation, and he, like Chris, stopped short when he saw the figure of Major Linkman on the floor. Then he approached and kneeled and turned Linkman over. There was a small hole in the temple, which was oozing blood. The face was peaceful, stronger in death than it must have been in life. There was even a smear over the sandy mustache, and the man's eyes were closed.

The trader rose, and over his bony face was a grim expression as he looked at Chris. "How did it happen?"

"We three were in the other part of the house," Chris said swiftly. "We heard the shot and ran to the office. He—he was lying just like that."

"Nothing been disturbed?"

"Nothing," Chris lied faintly, and turned away from the sight.

Hours later, when Mrs. Linkman's grief had worn itself out into sleep, Sylvia and Chris returned to their room, exhausted but wakeful, and undressed for bed. The agency doctor was sitting up with Mrs. Linkman.

Once the lamp was out they lay side by side, sleepless, and Chris's mind was a torment of fear. Why had she ever taken the glove? Would it not be better to turn it over to the authorities and let justice take its course against Ben, as it inevitably would? But she shrank from the thought of doing this, and immediately sought excuses. Yet if she didn't, she would be shielding the worst kind of murderer. And if she did, she would betray her own flesh and blood. Besides, couldn't someone who had Ben's glove have left it here? She didn't know, but she wished desperately that she had someone to whom she could turn now for advice. Not Sylvia, for she understood none of this. Not Doctor Benbow, for he admitted being prejudiced against Ben. And then she thought of Pete Yard. He would tell her, and tell her truly. Moreover, he might know if Ben was guilty.

Suddenly Sylvia's voice said in the dark, "Are you asleep?"

"No."

"Who could have done this awful thing to Major Linkman?"

"I don't know," Chris murmured. "The Indians?"

"But they liked him—as well as Indians ever like a white man." She was silent a while, and then said abruptly, "Pete would know."

Chris turned to look at her, but Sylvia's face was indistinct. "That's queer," Chris said gently. "I was thinking the same thing."

Sylvia felt for Chris's hand and took it in hers, then laughed a little. "We should hate each other, Christina. But I don't hate you. I like you." She hesitated. "Do you want to hear more about Pete—about what I know of him?"

And till long into the night Sylvia talked about herself and Pete. It was only then that Chris learned Sylvia's last name. Senator Waranrode, then, must be that "Little Lord God I worked for over yonder" that Pete mentioned the night at Doctor Benbow's. And Waranrode must in some way that Chris did not understand be connected with this trouble, else why would Pete want Sylvia away? But Chris listened quietly until Sylvia paused in her talking and asked gently, "Are you awake, Chris?"

There was no answer. Chris's breathing was smooth and deep.

Slowly Sylvia raised herself up on her elbow to look at this woman beside her, and then she sighed faintly in the dark and turned over to a sleep long in coming.

CHAPTER TWELVE

TEN TROUGHS, inevitably, was waiting for something. Since Sheriff Nance had disappeared, Ben Mellish, dark fury driving him, had directed the hunt. Townsmen were conscripted, as well as the Anchor and other riders. Weary horsemen came and went at all hours, but there were fewer people on the streets. Jim Bonal, the part-time deputy, like Ben Mellish, rode with them until weariness halted him, and then he slept in a chair on the porch of the Exchange House. But Ben Mellish sat awake beside him, cursing and impotent and domineering.

The quietest place in the town was the Legal Tender saloon, four doors down from the feed corral. It was a small place, catering mostly to the small ranchers at the north end of the Basin. Men rode its back alley furtively by night, and there was little heavy drinking done in its narrow, long room. Grim men watched the street from its wide front window and smiled and said little. Tonight Ed Briedehoff was one of them. He was content to wait, for Swan Ullman still held his place. Ben Mellish, wise enough to know that a part-time deputy is a poor substitute for a sheriff, had not made his brag good, and Ed, for a solid day now, had watched this activity with increasing amusement.

He stood behind the window of the Legal Tender now, just beyond reach of the batwing doors, and watched a band of riders come in from the south and dismount wearily in front of the Exchange House.

Miles Leston, beside him, said, "They oughta be tired of that soon."

"Not as long as Ben is still on his feet."

They smoked in comfortable silence a moment and then Ed said, "Where you reckon he took him?"

"If I know this Yard, I'd say Nance was in a shack right here in town."

Ed allowed himself a rare smile. "If he knew anyone here, that'd likely be true. He can ride a man."

Doc Benbow passed in front of the window and stepped through the swing doors.

"Evenin', Doc," Ed said, and Leston also greeted him, for in Doc Benbow they recognized a friend and godfather of half the babies in their end of the Basin.

Doc slacked against the bar, hat pushed back off his forehead, and chatted quietly with the bartender while he had his drink. Then he approached Ed and Miles, and watched the men scattered along the railing of the Exchange House listening to Ben Mellish.

"They don't seem to have much luck," Doc observed mildly.

"Good luck for us," Ed said.

Doc nodded. He said, without raising his voice, "I've got something up at my place I think you'd like to see, both of you."

Ed shot a hard, questioning glance at him, but Doc, his face morose and a little flushed, was on his way out.

Ed and Miles gave him five minutes and then went out the back way and got their horses. They rode down the alley to the cross street and turned up it and crossed the main street and went on back to Doc's place, dismounting in the alley and tying their horses back in the dark.

It was to the back door they went. Ed knocked on the door, and Doc opened it immediately, and Ed and Miles stepped into the kitchen, squinting against the sudden light.

Steve Trueblood and Pete Yard were seated on the other side of the big table.

Ed remembered how he had left Pete, and he nodded

to Steve and said to Pete, "A man hadn't ought to be as suspicious as I am, Yard."

"Forget it," Pete said, and indicated chairs, which Ed and Miles took.

Doc said musingly from the middle of the room, "If I don't hear anything, I can't tell anything, can I?"

"You, too, Doc," Pete said. "You've earned a hand in this."

"That's a promise?" Doc asked, sitting down, and Pete nodded.

"Then where is Nance?" Doc said. "That's been worryin' me. A hundred men in two days can pretty well look over this country."

Pete told them, adding, "Tonight he's loose—but without a horse. If he has any luck he'll be in town tomorrow. And that may be too late."

Ed watched him closely. "Too late?" he said mildly.

Steve interrupted gently, "Ed, who's been on the run now for a month?"

"We have."

"Who's on the run now?"

Ed smiled narrowly. "Ben is."

"You want to keep him that way?"

Ed looked sharply at him. "Maybe that ain't just right," he said in qualification. "Maybe he ain't on the run. Maybe he's just waitin' before he puts us on the run again."

"He is waiting," Steve conceded. "You aim to let him start in again as soon as Nance gets back?"

"Short of us takin' Nance again, I don't see how we can stop him," Leston said.

Pete settled his chair on all four legs and leaned across the table and tapped it with blunt forefinger. "The trouble with you," he said slowly, "is that you don't think Ben Mellish will scare."

"He won't," Ed said.

"What if Nance comes down here tomorrow and tells Ben Mellish to take his fight away from the sheriff's office, that he can ride high, wide and handsome just so long as he can make it stick? What if Nance does that?"

Ed turned this over in his mind and then he said carefully, "You know somethin', Yard?"

Pete smiled briefly. "Nance did a lot of thinkin' down there in that pit. He even got to askin' questions."

"Like what?"

"Like askin' me if there was any reason why I should have a five-thousand-dollar reward on my head. I said no. Like askin' if I didn't think a prejudiced lawman was worse than no law at all. I said yes to that."

Presently Ed said, "It don't sound like Nance."

Pete leaned back and waited. He remembered that Ed had told him Steve's meeting had come to nothing, which meant each of these men was on his own. Collectively they might have applauded the kidnaping of Sheriff Nance, but they would never act collectively to take advantage of it. He could see the caution on Ed's face, which was a sort of preliminary warning that he would not engage to fight Ben Mellish on behalf of his neighbors. And Pete did not blame him, although he did not intend to say or show it. He was waiting to see how Ed would accept this news of Nance's possible neutrality.

"If what you say about Nance is true," Ed said carefully, "then Ben Mellish may scare."

Pete said quickly, flatly, "But not from sheep."

Ed laid his hard, curious gaze on Pete. "Now you say what we come to listen to."

Pete grinned faintly. "You've got Mellish stopped now. When Nance comes back and tells him he's got to carry this fight on his own shoulders, Ben Mellish may be mad—but he'll do it, if you let him."

"And how will we stop him?"

Pete laid a hand gently on the table and said, "By carryin' the fight to him."

Ed sucked on his pipe. "We ain't organized, Pete."

"This'll take four men—no more."

"What will?" Leston asked.

Pete said, "Mellish hasn't even a skeleton crew at the Anchor. His whole outfit, outside the cook and horse wranglers, are out huntin' Nance. He—"

"I'm rustlin' no beef," Ed said flatly. "He stole none of mine."

"He's got three sheds of hay up there—two hundred tons," Pete said quietly, ignoring Ed's interruption.

Ed's face was impassive. Leston shifted faintly in his seat.

"Burn it," Pete said.

And before either of them could object, Pete leaned forward and said savagely, "Damn you two! You sit there lettin' the sky be pulled down on your heads because Ben Mellish hasn't moved against you yet! Don't you know what he'll do when Nance casts him off? He'll raid and burn and bushwhack and forget he ever knew Nance or the law, because he's the only man who knows how little Nance counts for. You're sittin' on dynamite now! The only way to do anything is get there first!"

Steve said quietly, "Two hundred tons of hay for the Utes at ten dollars a ton will bring two thousand dollars to hire more gunmen. He's got fifteen now. You Basin ranchers are twenty men, with twenty places to guard. If you don't make the fight, you're gone."

Doc, listening, turned his head, then rose, saying, "Hold it down" and went into his office. They heard him open the door and a woman greet him.

Ed Briedehoff glared balefully at both Pete and Steve. He said, "It strikes me you've got nothin' at stake, like we have."

Pete said contemptuously, "You haven't got anything at stake if you won't fight for it."

Doc appeared in the door. "Step in a moment, Pete."

Pete rose and turned his hard stare down on Ed and Miles, whose face was flushed with anger. "You can't bushwhack a law court. Remember that when you're run off your places and then try to win them back in court."

He stepped past Doc into the office and was face to face with Chris. Doc closed the door behind them.

"Why—what's the matter, Pete? Are you angry with me?" Chris asked.

The light in Pete's eyes faded and he shook his head. "You know I'm not. I'm—I'm tired of buttin' my head against a wall." He gestured to the sofa. "Sit down, Chris."

Chris reached inside her blouse and pulled out the glove and handed it to Pete. "I wanted to ask your advice, Pete. I don't know where to turn."

Pete accepted the glove and looked at it and said, "Ben's?"

"You've seen it?"

"No. But a man who has a palm burn would likely cut out that place. Besides, I never saw a bigger one."

Chris met his curious gaze and said, "Major Linkman was murdered in his office last night at the reservation."

"Murdered?" Pete said huskily. His lips were drawn tight over his teeth, and in his eyes was that same look that Chris had noticed the first night she saw him, a look of hot and savage anger. He turned away from her and walked over to Doc's window and suddenly he paused and looked blankly at the glove she had given him.

"What is this?" he asked, coming back to her.

"I picked that glove up by the body."

Pete looked at the glove and then said quietly, "Ben didn't do it."

"Are you sure?"

Pete only shook his head and said, "No. Not sure. But there are men here who could swear he didn't."

"Truthfully?"

"He's been hunting me for two days."

Chris sat down on the sofa and Pete, towering above her, watched the top of her head. "I want you to have it," Chris said.

Pete's somber face took on a cruel and ruthless cast then, but it was only fleeting. Slowly he scrubbed his chin with the flat of his hand, eyes speculative. Then he handed the glove back. "No, I won't frame him, Chris. Not even if he deserves it, as Ben does."

"But he didn't do it, you told me," Chris said swiftly, making no move to take the glove.

"He couldn't have."

"Then somebody wanted the authorities to believe he did."

Pete regarded her with close and watchful attentiveness as he said, "What of that?" In Chris's face he could see the struggle that was in her mind behind the shame and hesitancy she showed. She rose now and stood before him.

"This isn't honest, Pete, but maybe it will work. Take the glove and give it to Ben, nobody else. Maybe he'll believe then that his men are betraying him. For it must have been his men! And if he believes it, then maybe he will stop this quarrel. He will see he can't win it!"

"Ben will?" Pete murmured dryly. "You really think that, Chris—knowing Ben?"

Her glance fell and she shrugged. "No, I don't. But there's a chance. A slim one. And—and it's *got* to stop him, Pete!" she said vehemently.

"Maybe."

"Will you do it? Can you do it? Because if you and nobody else does it, he will see that you know and understand this treachery that will destroy him. If I did it he would threaten to kill me if I told you. But you can give it to him as if you could afford to be magnanimous, as if you didn't need to give it to Nance or the army authorities because you know he is doomed already. Can you do it?"

"Some way," Pete said. He laid a hand on her arm and said, "Why did you give this to me, Chris? How do you know I won't turn it over to the army investigator? I could. I hate Ben enough to do it."

"You are fair," Chris said.

Pete's hand withdrew and he rammed the glove in his hip pocket as he turned to the door. Then he paused and asked, "Does anyone else here know about Linkman's death?"

"I don't think so. Sylvia and I rode from daylight straight through."

"Sylvia?" Pete asked, after a moment's hesitation. He started back toward her. "Is she here?"

"Yes."

"I told her to stay at the reservation. Why didn't she?"

Pete asked harshly.

"We brought Mrs. Linkman with us. They are both at the hotel."

"Why did she come?" Pete asked angrily.

"To be near you." When Pete only stared at her, Chris added simply, "She loves you, Pete."

His gaze fell. Slowly, with the toe of his boot, he described a half-circle on the floor, and then he looked up at her. "It was never of my making," he said. Then he added, "Will you keep this quiet about Linkman as long as you can?"

Chris nodded, and Pete stepped back into the kitchen, closing the door behind him, and Chris stood motionless, remembering what he had said, "It was never of my making." Then he did not love Sylvia. She stepped out the door into the night, feeling her heart suddenly light, and she was smiling at something she could not have named.

Pete closed the door on a grim and waiting silence, and settled his gaze on Ed Briedehoff, for he did not want to look at Steve. Bitterly he remembered that if he had not stubbornly insisted on coming back to Ten Troughs to carry this war to Ben Mellish, Steve and he would have gone to Major Linkman. A threat to disclose his obvious connection with Waranrode might have brought the whole story tumbling from the major's lips. At worst, they would have made sure that that source of information was closed to them. And now the chance was gone, simply because he had been stubborn; and forever after Steve would blame him.

He said to Ed, with that anger and disgust bred from his thoughts, "You still here?"

Ed's jaw clamped a little more tightly on his pipe. "You're a hard man, Pete, and I don't know who you're hardest on—your friends or your enemies."

Steve said with quiet exultation, "It's settled, Pete. We're all going."

Pete smiled thinly and picked up his hat. "I'll be gone a few minutes. I'll meet you on the south road outside of town."

Letting himself out the back way, Pete turned into the alley and at the mouth of it, paused and looked up and down street, then hurried across to the mouth of the opposite alley.

The glove was in his hip pocket, a precious wedge that he would use to drive in between Ben Mellish and his arrogance. But that could wait. He thought of Chris giving it to him, and pity for her stirred deep within him. But she was a woman who needed no pity, he knew—a woman with a quiet and sturdy courage who would be cherished by a man some day in spite of this blight her brothers had spread over this land.

And it seemed strange to hear from her lips what he had always known about Sylvia, and what he had built against these years he had known her. Proud and fine as she was, she was not for him, nor were even her ways. He had watched Sylvia grow from a girl into a woman and he had seen that her life could never be his. He had tried to save her from this, and tonight he must, whatever happened.

At the rear of the hotel he paused and looked at it. There were steps there leading up to a door, which he guessed would open onto the through corridor into the lobby.

He tried it and found it open and let himself in and waited there, peering through its length into the dim-lighted lobby beyond. Out on the porch, he knew, Ben Mellish might be sitting yet, the hard and swearing wrath of his voice cursing his men and theirs and his own impotence. Too, as when he had looked earlier in the evening from across the street, his riders might be ringed around him, so that they had only to look up and through the window to see him. Only five men out of those fifteen Anchor riders would know him, and perhaps only three would recognize him as he walked through the circle of overhead light and to the desk to inquire from the clerk of Sylvia's room.

It was a chance he had to take. He tramped down the long corridor, making no pretence of stealth, swung into the lobby, and, cutting across the circle of light and out of it, he turned his face toward the stairs and looked up. And then he was out of the line of vision of a man on the porch, against a corner of the counter, talking to the middle-aged clerk.

"A dark girl," he said, "dressed in green, maybe. Did she register here tonight?"

The clerk looked at his register and said, "Sylvia Waranrode."

"That's the one. What number is her room?"

"Ten. Say, she ain't the senator's daughter, is she?"

"Senator?" Pete asked, and the clerk made a gesture of dismissal and Pete went up the stairs. At the top he paused and waited, watching the desk below. In the three minutes he stood there nobody came in to confer with the clerk, and Pete traveled the corridor, watching the doors.

He knocked at number ten, and it was immediately opened to him, and he stepped through, taking off his hat, as Sylvia shut the door.

Looking at her, it came to him that she was beautiful, and then thinking behind thought, he wondered that he had not noticed this about Chris, for she was even more beautiful than Sylvia.

Sylvia said, "She found you, I see. How?"

Pete said brusquely, "Why did you come back?"

Long ago Pete had shamed Sylvia from gracious evasion into the bluntness and honesty he practiced himself, and she had learned this lesson well. So she said, hand still on the door, "Didn't she tell you?"

"Yes. Sit down."

But Sylvia only walked over to him, a faint smile on her face. "I've grown up, Pete. I'm not a girl any more."

She came close and stood before him, smiling up at him, and desire stirred within him as he caught the fragrance of her.

He said quietly, "Don't kick a man when he's down. Sit down, I said."

Sylvia sat on the bed, and Pete followed her and sat beside her, and rolled a smoke and lighted it and then tendered her his sack of tobacco, which she took. While she expertly rolled a cigarette and while he lighted it for her, he regarded her with a kind of aloof fondness.

"That's something I never taught you," he said gruffly, "or I would never have drawn time on G.W. for three years."

"You taught me to relish my vices like a man, anyway," Sylvia said, laughing a little.

Pete felt easier now, and the two of them smoked in silence for a minute. Pete finally said, "This is going to be hard."

"Not if I can help it, Pete," Sylvia murmured, her voice purposely flat and matter-of-fact. "I love you. I've loved you ever since the day you rode into the place and took your own damn time looking it over before you asked for the job." She looked at him now. "I guess you've known that all along, only you were a little afraid of the Maid in the Castle. Or was that it?"

"You know it wasn't," Pete said.

"I guess not. Well, I love you. I've wanted you so long and so much **that** I can't ever remember when I didn't. I love you so much that I'm humble before you and—"

Gently Pete's hand closed over her mouth, and he left it there several seconds, his eyes bleak and strange. Then he took his hand away.

Immediately Sylvia said, "Pete, if you want me, take me now." She didn't even look at him. "I'm through. That's all I wanted to tell you."

Pete got off the bed and swung across the room and then came back and stood before her, his eyes hot and his lips pale. He leaned a hand on the bedpost and said sharply, "I tell it to you this way because you think like me, Sylvia. I want you, too—part of me—but it's no good. It won't work. And if you can talk and think like a man, you can take this like a man. You're not for me. I want sweat and fire smoke and rain and rope burns and raw whisky with my belly up to a bar. I want ten kids. I want to fight and swear at a horse and—"

"You always will," Sylvia said.

Pete straightened up and glared at her and then he said

with surprising mildness, "Yes. I always will want that. And you won't, will you?"

"No," Sylvia said, "—damn it!"

"Good," Pete said. "And now, for the last time, you listen to me. You get out of here. Get your horse and ride back to the reservation and—"

"Pete, is it Chris?"

"Is it—" Pete paused, gazing blankly at her. "Chris?" he murmured.

"She loves you. Do you love her?" And before Pete had a chance to answer, Sylvia sprang up and faced him. "No! Don't tell me! I don't even want to know."

She stood looking at him a full moment, looking at his face and eyes and hair as if she had hungered for them always. Then she said, "Pete, will you kiss me? I know. But let me be a woman just once. Will you kiss me?"

Pete folded her into his arms, and for one brief moment he felt the drug of her beauty and desire rioting through him, and then he reached up and pulled her arms from around him and picked up his hat and let himself out into the corridor. For a moment he stood there blindly, and then he tramped down the corridor to the stairs.

He was at the foot of them, walking almost drunkenly, turned into the corridor again, when he heard a yell from the porch and then on the echo of it there was a shot and a crash of glass.

He half-whirled, hearing Ben Mellish's wild roar, "Yard! Get him!"

Pete ran down the corridor, and then in its welcome darkness he wheeled through a door and ran for the black slot of window across the room. He crashed into something and cursed, and above it he could hear the tramp of feet in the lobby.

Quickly he threw the window open and looked out. Between the buildings he could see men running toward the rear of the hotel.

The first man approached and pounded past and several others followed. Crouching to the side of the window, Pete heard one say, "Watch those windows."

Men were in the corridor now, and he could hear them out in back calling to each other. Standing utterly still in that dark room, he knew that unless he could make his way back through the corridor he was caught. Carefully he stepped across to the door and inched it open. Just outside the door, looking up toward three punchers close to the lobby, was a townsman with a gun in his hand. Over this man's shoulder Pete saw two of these men go into the dining-room, and he could hear them tramp its length, working toward him. On the back steps Ben Mellish's voice bellowed, "Work those sheds over and kick up that fire, Blake!" Then it was louder, as if he turned to shout down the corridor, "Stay where you are, you two!"

The murmur of voices below the side window did not let up. He could see the crack of light penciled under the door to the dining-room shrink as the lamp came nearer, and he knew that in a moment that door would open and only a gun would win him freedom. He did not want that.

He swung the door to the corridor open and tapped the townsman on the shoulder, saying, "Easy. Here is my gun."

The townsman lunged away from this voice at his back and swiveled his gun around, firing it into the wall, and still Pete did not move, so that the man looked sheepish, then yelled, "Mellish! Mellish!"

"Take my gun," Pete said. "In my belt."

Cautiously the man reached out and took his gun, and Pete stepped in the corridor as Ben Mellish bulked through the door, and then walked slowly toward him. From all sides Anchor men gathered.

"Get up front," Ben commanded crisply.

Under the lobby light Ben paused, and Pete stopped and faced him. Ben's eyes were swollen and bloodshot from sleeplessness and his voice was hoarse. He said to the townsman, "That's five thousand, George," but he wasn't looking at the townsman; he was smiling meagerly at Pete.

"That was cuttin' it a little too fine, even for you, Yard," Ben said.

"Looks that way, doesn't it?" Pete murmured.

"Come along."

There was an escort of some twenty men as far as the sheriff's office. Jim Bonal, who had slept through the shooting and the shouting in his chair on the porch, was dragged to his feet and carried along until he was sufficiently awake to walk by himself. At the sheriff's office Pete was prodded in behind Bonal, and Ben shut the others—except Blake, his foreman—out into the night.

He did not waste time now. "Where is Nance?" he demanded, and Pete told him. Obligingly he even related the kidnaping, and he cruelly observed Ben Mellish's face flush with new anger.

"So he'll be down here tomorrow?" Ben asked, suspicion in his voice.

"If he has luck. If you want him, send a man up with a horse."

"Why did you turn him loose?"

"You haven't moved in on Swan Ullman, have you?"

Ben said thickly, "No, but I will."

"I doubt it. You lost your chance to make that stick, Ben. It won't work again."

Blake cleared his throat and lounged off the desk and walked over and hit Pete in the face. It was poor judgment, besides being a poor blow, for Pete rolled with it enough to catch it glancing on his cheekbone, and he drove his fist squarely and thought-fast into Blake's face. Blake caromed off the desk and into the wall and fell, and Ben Mellish regarded him with a kind of savage scorn.

Pete murmured, "I didn't know you bought that kind of loyalty for fightin' wages."

Jim Bonal said irritably, "That's enough of this! What you want done with him, Ben?"

"Lock him up," Ben said.

The jail was a stone affair of four small cells, and its entrance was through a door in the back wall of the tiny office. Jim Bonal went ahead with the keys and the lantern and opened a cell for Pete, who went in.

"Leave that lantern," Pete said quietly. "I want a word

with Mellish."

Bonal looked at Ben, who nodded curtly, and Bonal left.

Pete drew the glove from his pocket and handed it to Ben, saying, "Remember where you left that, Ben?"

Ben took the glove and turned it over and then looked darkly at Pete. "You haven't been over there."

"Waranrode's?"

"Yes."

Pete shook his head, watching Ben Mellish closely as he said, "Have you heard Major Linkman, the Ute agent, was killed last night?"

"No," Ben said carefully.

Pete gestured to the glove. "That was found beside his body."

Ben's frown washed out a little and he looked sharply at Pete and took a step toward him. "That's a lie," he said flatly.

"From what I've heard," Pete said gently, "you've called your sister a lot of things, Mellish, but you've never called her a liar. She was at Linkman's last night when he was shot. She found that glove beside him, and she hid it. If she hadn't it would have gone with you just the way somebody hoped it would."

Ben said nothing, but his eyes were wary, puzzled.

"Keep it," Pete said idly. "In your place, I'd tie it around my neck, so that every time I touched it, it would tell me that I'd gone out on the limb just a little too far— and that the man who put me out there never even aimed to let me get back."

Ben said harshly, quickly, "This is your frame-up!"

"Frame-up?" Pete echoed. "Talk sense. You've got the glove. I could have turned it over to the army men who'll be here in a few days, and they could have questioned Chris to find out the truth." He shook his head. "It's no frame-up, Ben—not mine, anyway. You figure out whose it is. You know where you left the glove. You know where it was found."

Then Ben Mellish cursed in passionate abandon, and

Pete watched him idly, reminded of a stupid bear who is cornered and will not admit it. When Ben was finished, Pete drawled, "This Basin will be a tough outfit to buck alone, Ben. Waranrode knew that, counted on it."

Mellish glared at him and then swung on his heel and went out. Pete lay down on the cot and listened idly to the talk out in the office, which was only an indistinct blur to him. Thinking back over his capture, he had a feeling of unaccountable anger at his clumsiness and lack of caution. And for that he had to thank his own weak and willful way with Sylvia. He had left her, his mind and body tormented with wanting her, and he had stumbled into this trap. A man in his senses would have left by the back stairs or a window.

He rolled a smoke in the dark, trying to put these thoughts behind him.

In a very short time he heard Steve's voice out in the office, raised in violent protest—probably because he was not allowed to see Pête. And Pete hoped desperately that the guard would not tell Steve of Linkman's murder, in case Ben had not kept it a secret. For Pete was sure that when Steve heard of Linkman's death he would name their fight as a useless thing, doomed to failure. Perhaps he would not quit, for Steve was a stubborn man; but he would leave this Basin war for Washington, where he would demand an investigation on the little evidence they had assembled, and probably in vain. To Pete, who knew that in Steve lay the ability to kindle this war, a withdrawal now would mean defeat. It would leave Waranrode the time he needed to get rid of Mellish, just as he had rid himself of Linkman. No, this fight had to flare up, had to be brought into the open, had to breed a violence that would crack it open clear down to Waranrode. But how it was to be done Pete didn't know.

And soon Pete even stopped thinking of that, for he was remembering what Sylvia said about Chris. "She loves you, Pete. Do you love her?" Many long minutes he lay utterly still, feeling for the cause of Sylvia's saying that. It was not true, he was sure; it was the hysteria of the moment and the circumstances. For Chris did not love him. When she had held the gun on Ames that was only the hatred of seeing a man murdered. That night when he had lied to Sylvia, holding Chris's arm, she had hated him. Tonight she came to him in desperation, with only the courageous hope that he might be able to save Ben. Never in anything Chris had ever said or done was there any justification for Sylvia's saying that. And wearily Pete hated this because it was so. No woman had the power to make him aware of her as Chris did. And he knew now, for the first time, that it was partly Chris who had brought him back to this Basin fight. It was because behind this madness of Ben Mellish's, bred by Waranrode, Pete could see that Chris was doomed as certainly as Ben, and that he would pull her down with him—and by her own choice. Deep within her, she was too loyal to quit Ben, so that when vengeance was visited on him she would share it.

And again Pete had no answer for this, knowing that if he was to save her it would only be by destroying Ben before he could pull her with him. And that, Chris would never forgive.

CHAPTER THIRTEEN

BONAL HAD BROUGHT him his breakfast hours ago, and Pete had smoked until his mouth was dry before he heard the deep rumble of Ben Mellish's voice out in the office. It was not gentle this morning, and while Pete was trying to catch the tenor of his conversation he heard Nance's voice, too. It broke off suddenly and the jail door swung open and Nance entered. He was unshaven and bits of dirt and leaves still clung to his clothes. Ben Mellish was behind him, wearing that harried truculence on his face that had lately become a part of him.

Steve Trueblood, homely and silent and watchful, came last.

Pete looked at each of them as Ben reached out and whirled Nance around to face him. Steve looked back into the office and then stood beside the door, his hand on his gun.

Ben said, "Nance, I've got twenty men out there that will cut him to doll rags the minute he steps out of that office!"

"That," Nance said flatly, unpleasantly, "is bluff."

Steve drawled, "If they try it, you'd better be clean out of sight, Mellish."

Ben watched with a kind of fascinated rage as Nance put the cell key up to its lock. Then Ben backed against the bars, swiftly drawing his gun, so that its small arc covered both Nance and Steve.

"He stays in there," Ben said ominously. "Nance, you put out reward posters and five thousand dollars. If you've lost your mind, I reckon I haven't. You can't play with murder."

Nance gave one level look at Ben and he said abruptly, "You damn bullhead. Put up that gun or I'll have you in here next. I'm sheriff of this county, dead or alive, and I'm openin' this cell, dead or alive. If you think you can fight this town and the rest of this county on top of the whole north Basin, just let that thing off." And with easy unconcern he unlocked the cell door, and opened it. Without looking at Ben he said to Pete, "Come out. There's no charge against you."

Ben said thickly, "Stay in there!"

Nance swiveled his gaze at him. "Ben," he drawled gently, "put that up," and he walked toward Ben. It was a long two seconds. Stubborn and savage as Ben was, there was still a sanity in him, and behind the murderous rage in his eyes was caution—and fear.

When Nance stretched out his hand to take the gun, Ben lowered it, and he said simply, "You have started a thing you'll never finish now, Nance."

Nance nodded grimly. "Get into the office, the lot of you. I've got my speech to make yet."

When Pete had his gun again he stood beside the desk,

Steve a little behind him. Ben stood by the half-open door. Outside, still on their horses, Pete could see the Anchor riders waiting. Beyond them, and on the far sidewalk close to the Legal Tender, a little knot of silent, watchful men lounged. These were the Basin ranchers.

Nance sat down and talked to Ben. "For ten years, Ben, I thought Dave Mellish was doin' the wrong thing by lettin' those nesters settle on the bottom lands and prairie that he could rightfully claim. And when you started to do somethin' about it I backed you up." He pointed a blunt finger at Ben. "But I don't back up any man's steal—even if he's a United States senator."

Pete was grinning faintly when Ben's hot gaze shuttled to him.

Nance went on. "If you'd fought for this land for yourself, I might have overlooked the way you went about it. Even if you'd taken this land into a company and let the court settle it, I might have thought that was a little cheaper than hirin' riders for ten years to back up your fence. But my blood or not, I'll not back you up when you steal it for a crook."

Ben said sneeringly, "Then you've swung over to that nester rabble?"

"I haven't swung anywhere," Nance said grimly, "except back to plumb center. I won't promise to settle all the trouble that goes on in this Basin, but I can promise you this—I'll worry hell out of the man that steps out of line!"

"Maybe you'd like to start on the outfit that burned two hundred tons of my hay last night," Ben said darkly.

Steve shifted faintly, and Pete did not look at him.

"I will," Nance said. "If you've got a legal complaint, you bring it to me."

Ben laughed softly, without mirth. "I won't bring anything to you, Nance. I've brought the last thing to you I ever will—except a pack of trouble." He looked up then at Pete. "You made a poor choice, Yard. In jail you might have lived."

"Which might be said for you, Ben," Pete murmured.

"When you're not certain of that, remember that glove."

Ben left, closing the door behind him, and there was movement among the riders outside.

Steve's homely face was set in a frown and he was observing Pete as Nance rose and watched from the window.

"What glove?" Steve said curiously.

"Ben Mellish's. Somebody planted it by Linkman the other night when they shot him."

Nance turned abruptly. "Linkman? Major Linkman killed?"

"Shot."

Steve directed a long, wondering, bitterly reproving look at Pete and then walked over to the window beside Nance and looked out.

"Well," Steve said mildly, furiously. "So that's where we end up? Right where we began. No, behind that."

"I wonder," Pete murmured.

Steve half-turned and looked at him and then picked up his hat and without a word walked to the door.

"Hold on," Nance said. "I'm tellin' you two exactly what I told Ben. The first one of you that cuts loose his dogs in this Basin has got me to reckon with."

Steve didn't bother to answer. He stepped out onto the walk, and Pete followed. Bitterly Steve regarded the sunny street, and without a word he swung under the hitchrack and headed for the Legal Tender.

Inside, at the bar, he said to the bartender, "I want the biggest bottle of the reddest paint you've got," and when he got the whisky he chose a table in a far corner. Pete sat down beside him and Steve poured out two drinks, but before he drank his he said accusingly, "You knew about Linkman last night. You knew before you sent Ed and Leston and me up to the Anchor to burn that hay."

"Yes."

Steve didn't look at him. He continued stubbornly, "Why did you do it? I don't mind it for myself, Pete, but you should never have sent those other two up there, knowing what you did about Linkman—because our fight is busted. Linkman was the only man we could have reached to get evidence on Matt Waranrode. And Linkman is dead. And all the fighting we do now is water that should be under the bridge."

Pete listened with head bowed, eyes musing, toying with his glass of whisky.

"Because, old son, we're licked," Steve said wearily. "Waranrode is a thorough man. Without our lifting a finger, he'll take care of Mellish. But not before Ben Mellish burns and bushwhacks those poor devils till they curse the day they saw us."

Pete sipped his whisky in silence, not looking at Steve.

"Ed was right," Steve murmured. "You're a hard man, Pete—harder on your friends than on your enemies."

Pete flushed a little and his mouth drew tight, and still he toyed with his glass, silent. Steve rose and laid a hand on Pete's shoulder and said, "Let me blow off. It's not every day a man loses a fight like that." He walked up to the bar and said something to the bartender, who extended him a box of cigars. Steve took a handful and rammed them in his shirt pocket and came back and sat down. He laid one beside Pete. "One for you. Five for me. By the time I'm finished with the last one, carry me over to the Exchange House and put me to bed."

Slowly Pete turned his head and saw Steve touch a match to his cigar. And not so slowly Pete reached over and took it out of his mouth and broke it, rising half out of his seat, throwing the cigar on the floor. He said to Steve in a choked voice, "I have made many a wrong guess about men in my life, Steve, but I always claimed I could see the yellow on a man's back through his clothes. I reckon I'll back down on that claim, here and now, because up till now I missed seein' yours." He rose and placed both square hands on the table and leaned toward Steve, and his somber face was savage with anger. "I can carry this alone. And when I can't, you can sit down to that printin'-press of yours and lay out in type, 'Here dies a man that tried to finish what he started!'"

Steve rose out of his chair so quickly that it tumbled over backward. And Pete, straightening up with him, was suddenly aware that this room packed with men had fallen silent. But it was not the silence of men who are watching a brewing fight; it was a motionless, flat, and warning silence, and instantly Pete swiveled his head.

Tim Blake, tough and arrogant and disdainful, stood just within the door of the Legal Tender. He saw Pete, and he started toward him, ignoring every other man in this room. Six feet from Pete he stopped, and the lip-lifted sneer on his hard-muscled face was more vicious than his voice as he said, "Yard, Ben says your boys have called the turn. The next time I see you, it'll be keno. And if you want to make it this time, I'll take that up, too."

Pete's hand was not an inch from his glass of whisky. He looked down at it and picked it up and threw it in Blake's face. With a throaty laugh he lunged at the gunman.

There was no collision, only the slap of hard flesh on flesh as Pete's hand settled on Blake's wrist which was moving to lift that last inch of gun barrel clear of the holster top. Pete's laugh lay wild and throaty through the room.

Blake's shoulder sagged down under the driving twist of Pete's hand, and the gun clattered to the floor.

Pete's other hand had gathered Blake's vest and shirt into a tight-fisted wad, and heaving under with shoulder muscles corded, Pete lifted him clear of the floor. He hit him in the face, again and again and again—four times in all. Then, folding him over his shoulder, Pete strode past the bar and sent the swing-doors crashing aside. Never pausing in his stride, he straightened his burdened arm in a low, smooth roll that sent Blake clear of the hitchrack to thud into the soft dust of the street. It stirred around Blake as Pete raised his eyes to see Ben Mellish and his riders ringed in a silent group in the street.

Pete said thickly, "Too much talk, Ben. Will you take it now or wait?"

The anger in him was blind and raging, and its tautening violence seemed to lay a silence over the still noon air. "Speak up, man!"

Ben Mellish said quietly, "I'll wait." To one of his men

he said, "Pick the fool up."

Pete turned into the saloon. His blindness did not seem to take into account that behind the window these men had been watching this and that not even now did they ignore him for what was still in the street outside. He singled out Steve among them—Steve, who was closest to the door and who had his gun in his hand.

Pete said to him, "I'm not done with what I had to say. Steve, I'm ridin' out of here. I'll bring back what you want —Linkman or no Linkman. Then maybe you'll hang up your dress and listen."

He tramped out and up street into the feed stable, and a moment later rode out of town south.

From the street Steve saw him, and he swore long and fervently—and then sat down on the edge of the board-walk, because his knees were too unsteady to hold him.

CHAPTER FOURTEEN

THE SECOND DAY of riding put Pete almost across the Ute reservation, and on that afternoon he met a Ute buck and his two half-grown sons, who pointed out to him the southern reservation boundary. Beyond that would be Lassiter's Chevron range, and Pete was well into it by nightfall. He felt and knew himself to be a man alone now, for Steve was lost to him.

A stranger in these vast, mesa-shot Lowenweep Breaks, Pete had to move slowly, but by the next afternoon he had found a brush corral by a spring at the head of a box can-yon. That night, when a band of horses came to water there, Pete drove them into the corral. An hour later the first step of his plan was completed. From this band he had cut out a runty black gelding, shod, who still carried his winter coat of hair, arguing that he had not been ridden this spring. This gelding bore the Chevron brand on left hip and cheek.

Next morning, after Pete had prised the gelding's left-front shoe off, he headed across the breaks toward Wheeler, a cattle-shipping point on the transcontinental, and seat of Humboldt County. He was leading the black gelding, which, after a half day's travel over this rocky terrain, was lamed.

At Wheeler, Pete sought out the courthouse, which was converted from an old saloon and fronted on the wide and dusty road that paralleled the tracks. After a fifteen-minute conversation with Burke, the Humboldt County sheriff, they adjourned to the sidewalk, and while Pete remained silent Sheriff Burke looked at the black gelding.

Burke was past middle age, a shrewd-eyed, ruddy-faced man, who accepted Pete's information that he was Welch, a new deputy of Nance's, without any suspicion. He wore a black, flat-brimmed Stetson with a leather belt for a hatband, and now he cuffed it off his forehead.

"This is the pony, huh?"

Pete nodded.

"Lamed, you say?"

Again Pete nodded and said, "They found the shoe. I got it in my blankets."

"I'll be with you in a minute," Burke said, and went off to get his horse.

They rode the twelve miles to Lassiter's place in easy time, Pete leading the black gelding. The Chevron house squatted against the base of a bare red butte, and was a low, rambling affair of adobe, with a dirt roof and slab additions to either side of the long low porch. Pole corrals and sheds lay around it, and it had the sun-baked shadeless appearance of any dry-country ranch.

Approaching it, Sheriff Burke said, "I don't know Lassiter so good, but you let me talk."

Pete stirred himself out of his air of indifferent laziness long enough to agree.

Lassiter was working out in the corrals, and a shout from the cook brought him to the house. He was an angular, taciturn man of medium height and weight, with a straw-colored mustache, ragged and full, which hid what must have been a rather grim mouth. To Pete, who eyed him lazily, he might have been a retired ranch foreman.

Burke shook hands with him and introduced Pete, and then jerked a thumb toward the gelding whose lead rope was tied to the saddle of Pete's ground-haltered horse.

"Your horse, Jim?" Burke asked, and sat down on the porch. Pete followed suit. Lassiter walked over to the pony and looked at it and said, "He's wearin' my brand, ain't he?"

"Sure," Burke agreed. He gave Lassiter time to come back and sit down beside him and roll a smoke.

"Heard about Linkman over at the agency bein' murdered?" Burke asked innocently, watching Lassiter. The nod in reply was curt and indifferent.

"Shot," Burke murmured. "Funny thing." He smoked a while in silence, then said mildly, "You rode that horse lately, Jim?"

Lassiter shook his head. "He's no damn good. He's been runnin' loose since winter. Still carryin' most of his winter coat." He looked up at Burke. "Why?"

"That-there horse was tracked from Linkman's place out to somewhere in the reservation, where he throwed a shoe. Whoever rode him picked up a Ute pony and switched saddles and let that horse go. The fella that shot Linkman, I mean. He's the one that left the horse there."

Lassiter removed the cigarette from his mouth and turned his head toward Burke and said, "Who said so?"

Burke gestured to Pete. "Welch here is one of Ross Nance's deputies over in Ten Troughs. He'll tell you what he told me."

Lassiter gave Pete a searching glance, which Pete did not see, because he was lazily sifting sand through his fingers. He began to talk.

"This wasn't any of Nance's business. He figured it belonged to the army and they're sendin' a man up to work on it. But there's always a bunch of punchers loose that aim to solve the thing in two hours. It was a G.W. puncher and a couple of Utes that picked up the pony. They found the shoe he lost and then they found the pony and brought him to Nance."

"Why Nance?" Lassiter asked. "He don't have any say-so over the Ute reservation. And the G.W. ain't even in Ten Troughs country. It's fifty miles off on the other side of Rafts."

"You got me there," Pete murmured. "Nance didn't aim to do anything about it. He told this puncher to take it up with the army. But that was before this other thing happened. After that he figured, whether it was any business of his or not, Sheriff Burke ought to know."

"What other thing?" Lassiter said.

Pete glanced at Burke and Burke nodded. Pete said to Lassiter then, "Understand, I'm just repeatin' what was told to Nance."

"What?"

"Well, a day or so after Linkman was killed, a couple of Utes drifted into the agency. They'd been out roundin' up some horses and they hadn't heard about Linkman's murder. Hadn't heard about this black gelding, either. When they found out about it they remembered that they come across a white man on the reservation a day or so back. He didn't stop, and he didn't speak, but they thought they recognized the horse he was ridin'. It was a Ute horse."

"What about him?" Lassiter asked impatiently.

"The description they gave," Pete said quietly, "run like this: Middle age, not heavy and not tall, just medium. He had a cornsilk mustache, they said—pretty full, and sort of straw-colored."

Lassiter's cigarette had gone out. He dropped it now and looked steadily at Burke. "That pretty well fits me, don't it?"

Burke nodded. "Seemed so to me, Jim. When Welch give me the description it just naturally tied in with the brand on that horse there."

Lassiter put his elbows on his knees and looked off across the stretch of pasture in front of the house. "Happens I was here most of the last two weeks. Cook could prove that."

"I don't doubt it," Burke murmured. "Call him out,

will you?"

The cook answered Lassiter's yell, and he testified that Lassiter had taken most of his meals at the ranch house for the past two weeks—ever since Lassiter and one of his men had come back from cleaning out water holes and springs after the winter.

When the cook was gone Burke didn't say anything immediately. It was obvious to them all that if Lassiter had wanted to rig up a story he could have warned the cook to say just what he had.

Presently Lassiter said, "Those two Utes that claimed they saw me. They came in alone to tell Nance?"

Pete frowned as Lassiter turned to look at him. "No," Pete said slowly, "I don't think they did. I wasn't there when they come, but I recall Nance sayin' a man brought them."

"Remember his name?"

Again Pete frowned with the effort of memory. "Not exactly. Man by the name of Magersfield or Majorsfield or Agersfield or something like that."

"Manderfield—Ames Manderfield," Lassiter prompted.

"That's the name," Pete murmured.

"A G.W. rider, wasn't he?"

"That's right. A G.W. rider."

Lassiter smiled narrowly. "Seems like the G.W. took a lot of interest in gettin' Linkman's murderer."

Pete looked thoughtful as he shuttled his gaze to Lassiter. "It does, don't it? I recall one of them G.W. riders sayin' his boss and Linkman were good friends."

"Waranrode, you mean?"

"Yes. That would be the name."

No one spoke for a few moments. Burke said then, "I don't rightly know what to do about this, Jim. What do you think?"

"You're the sheriff," Lassiter said grimly.

"I know it. But it ain't any business of mine. Nance didn't call for an arrest. He just thought I ought to know about this pony. The army hasn't sent me word. I got no legal reason for holdin' you, especially on the say-so of a couple of Ute Indians."

"And the G.W. riders," Lassiter said dryly.

"And them. Still, if you was to dodge out after I'd gone, I'd look pretty silly, wouldn't I, when the army sent word to bring you over? And they'll do it, you can bet."

Lassiter spat in the dust and wiped his mustache and did not even look at Burke.

"It strikes me, Jim, you're goin' to have to do some talkin' some time soon," Burke went on.

Lassiter only nodded.

"You aim to do it?"

Lassiter said merely, "I'll tell the truth."

"Then why not go over and see Nance?" Burke suggested. "He'll likely be workin' with the man the army sends."

"Hell with the army," Lassiter said bitterly.

"All right. But it's goin' to look a lot better for you if you're right there to hear it all and put in your word. That is, unless you was the man that rode this black away from Linkman's. In that case, you're caught right now."

Lassiter stood up and walked over to the black and looked at him again. He came back and said to Pete, "I don't see no saddle marks on him."

"Neither do I," Pete said. "I never did. But he likely worked them off rollin'."

Lassiter said, "That horse could have been picked up on my range any time this winter and I'd never of missed him."

"Sure," Pete said.

Lassiter looked at him speculatively. "All right. I'll go," he said grimly. "I can't see through this thing, or around it, but I can smell it—and it stinks."

Pete didn't comment. Lassiter stomped into the house. Burke shifted his position so he could watch the door and he lifted his holster to his lap.

"That all right with you and Nance?" he asked Pete, and Pete nodded.

"Mind, I don't know this Lassiter," Burke went on. "He might be a hardcase for all I know. He might even wait till he gets out with you and then shoot you in the back."

"I'll take a chance," Pete murmured, and he smiled, but not at what Sheriff Burke thought.

Lassiter came out with his bedroll and a sack of grub, and saddled his horse. They mounted, and Burke, always a cautious man, suggested to Lassiter that he take the lead rope of the black gelding, which would have to be taken to Ten Troughs for evidence.

Burke rode west with them until the road to Wheeler turned south, and then Pete and Lassiter rode on together.

Lassiter was a taciturn man, and kept his silence most of the afternoon. At dusk, when they made camp at a spring deep in the Lowenweep Breaks, Pete took the horses to stake out while Lassiter made the fire and supper.

After they were finished, Pete sat on his blankets and smoked. Lassiter stared moodily at the fire, frowning.

Presently Lassiter said, "This G.W. rider, the one that found the black out on the reservation, what was his name?"

"Ames Manderfield."

Lassiter looked up sharply. "You never said that this afternoon."

"You never asked."

Lassiter had not ceased looking at Pete. He contemplated him now with a mixture of suspicion and surliness. "You know," he said finally, "I've got an idea you knew this Ames Manderfield all the time."

Pete said nothing. He rose and stretched and then put a hand on his gun and pulled it out and pointed it at Lassiter.

"Know him?" he murmured. "I work for him. I work for Waranrode, too—but Waranrode never said it would be this easy." He added, "Put your hands up."

Slowly Lassiter rose, and even more slowly raised his hands. He said quietly, "What is this?"

"Murder," Pete murmured. "At least those were Waranrode's orders."

CHAPTER FIFTEEN

THE ANCHOR RIDERS kept to the shoulder of the slope, riding the shadows beneath the deep timber in single file. Below them and far off they caught an occasional wink of a light in Miles Leston's place.

Blake, who was riding ahead, pulled up now and said to Ben Mellish, "Can we take to the road?"

"Go ahead," Ben said grimly. "Nance won't have to do any guessing anyway."

The dozen riders came out of the timber now to bunch on the road, Mellish at their head, and they walked their horses around the bend that gave them a clean view of the light in Swan Ullman's place on the other side of the high valley.

"He keep any dogs?" Blake murmured.

"No. What if he does?"

They rode on and quietly into the yard, and as they neared the house Swan came to the door, the lamp behind him outlining him.

"That you, Ed?" he asked mildly.

Ben Mellish did not answer immediately. He rode up close to the house and his men followed him.

"It's Mellish, Swan," Ben said. "We've come to take over."

Swan stood motionless a second, and then his hand moved to pick up the rifle beside the door. He said quietly to his wife inside, "You stay there." He stepped over the sill, carrying the rifle, and walked over to the spot from which Ben Mellish's voice had come.

"You're through in this Basin, Ben," Swan said patiently. "Even a man with as little sense as you got can see that. Nance has even dropped you."

Ben didn't say anything.

"There was a time—and not long back—when you pretty

much had your way with us. But don't try to take it now. You make one bad move and you'll kick up the kind of trouble you ain't lookin' for." Swan paused and waited for Ben to answer, but only the sound of the stomping of horses around him and the jingle of their bridle chains came to him. He added, still mildly, "Now ride off."

Turning he walked toward the house, back to the horse-men.

Ben Mellish murmured, "All right, Blake."

Swan caught the sound of the voice, and he paused, one foot on the sill, and half-turned, to face the flat hammer-ing of five gunshots. Dropping his rifle he spread both hands wide to catch the door jambs, and then he turned and lunged a step into the house and pitched to his knees. His wife's scream rang out into the night even as he fell.

Blake dismounted lightly and walked through the door, holstering his gun. Mrs. Ullman, her face twisted with terror, held a heavy Colt in her hand, and as Blake entered she fired it at him. Blake lunged for her and wrenched the gun out of her hand, and in spite of her fighting and claw-ing and kicking and sobbing dragged her by an arm out into the night, where one of the riders held her.

Then Blake returned with another rider, and they pro-ceeded to stack up the mean furniture in the middle of the floor. All except the table, for they laid Swan Ullman on that. There were two kerosene lamps burning against the night, one in a wall bracket, the other on the table. Blake knocked the chimneys off them and blew them out and smashed one on the pile of furniture. The other he bothered to unscrew and poured the contents over Swan Ullman's shirt and pants.

After he had touched a match to the furniture he came out. Mrs. Ullman sat on the hard-packed dirt, sobbing hysterically, and Blake stood by her, his hard face musing, until the flames caught and the heat became unbearable so close. She was moved away from it then. Other riders had killed the stock and fired the sheds.

Ben Mellish watched the fire take hold of the dry cabin logs until its light turned the small pocket of valley into day. Then he moved his horse over to Mrs. Ullman and reined up beside her.

"Tell the rest of Swan's nester friends how things are now," he said. Mrs. Ullman looked up at him, and in her eyes was all the unforgiving hate of a hard woman's soul. Ben laughed complacently and reined his horse away, and his riders dropped in behind him. Once clear of the valley they took to the timber again, this time cutting off toward Ed Briedehoff's.

When they came to Ed's place it was dark, and Ben rode cautiously up to the house and listened, hearing only quiet night sounds in the gray dark.

"Ed!" he said, and there was no answer. He called to Blake, "All right," and the Anchor crew moved into the yard. Blake and another rider dismounted and walked up to the porch. Off up the slope a rifle cracked sharply, and the man beside Blake grunted and tripped and fell. Then from this same place another and louder rifle joined the first.

Ben Mellish said sharply to Blake, "Get in there!" and he wheeled his horse toward the slope. "Come on!" he commanded the three remaining men, who were returning the fire now. The horse closest to Ben went down, his rider cursing wildly above the steady hammering of the two rifles up the slope. This rider caught up Blake's horse, and it immediately stampeded down off the shoulder of the knob, but Ben, who checked his horse and stood alone, utterly contemptuous of the rifle fire, yelled at the other two, "Damn you, come on!" It was his bold, hard voice, in seeming disregard of the shooting, that turned the men, and they spurred over to him and past him and raced up the slope into the brush, shooting blindly into the night. A riderless horse milled between them, sawing across their paths in terror, until the night was filled with Ben's snarling curses. There was no system; they fought their horses up the slope to the spot from which the shots had come, and these, almost unnoticed, had ceased now. When they reached the place they beat the brush back and forth, stopping to listen and to call to each other, but the riflemen had left.

Ben whistled them down to the shack. Checkup revealed another man missing besides the one who had gone down at the first shot.

Blake, who had leaned on a pillar of the porch during all this, lounged erect now and spat over the body at his feet.

"Touch the place off, and give us some light," Ben said darkly.

Blake followed the same procedure as at Ullman's. When the flames had crawled through the door and windows Ben sent his two men to catch up the two loose horses and to hunt for the remaining body. He was discovered just over the shoulder of the hill. He was dead when they brought him and laid him down before Ben.

It was with murky anger in his eyes that Ben Mellish regarded the two men at his feet. No pity roused it, for these men could be bought at a hundred a month and they knew the risk; it was a sullen rage that Ed Briedehoff and the other rifleman had successfully defied him. He touched the boot of one with his own foot and then looked up at Blake, who was chewing thinly on a cut of tobacco.

"Load them on their ponies. We'll take them back."

Blake detailed the others to this job with a quiet word. These two were silent now, a little sobered by what they had just witnessed, a little shamed by Ben Mellish's disregard of real danger.

Ben walked over to the dead horse and Blake trailed him. In that uncertain light Ben drew out his pocketknife and kneeled and cut out the square of hide from the horse's hip which held the brand. Then he gave it to Blake, saying, "Throw that in the fire."

Blake took it. "I thought this was in the open now."

"There's always Nance," Ben said harshly. "But he can't try a man without a body to prove a murder. And he can't prove a burning on us without evidence to show in court we did it."

Blake thought this over a moment, ruminating on the piece of wet hide he had in his hand. "What would you call Ullman's wife?" he said. "What would you call those two up on the slope?"

"Three people's word against myself and three of my own riders," Ben said briefly. "Get on."

Steve and Ed, from the height of the bare ridge beyond Ed's place, watched the shack go up in flames. The figures of the men clotted around the shack were small, but plain, and Ed watched them hunt for the body and saw Ben Mellish walk over to the dead horse and kneel by it.

He said quietly, "You got any shells left?"

"Rifle? No."

"Forty-five?"

"It's too far."

"Have you?"

"No."

Ed sighed. "It can wait," he said, and Steve said nothing. It came to him how thoroughly right Pete had been in damning him for a quitter. There was no quitting now, and one look at Ed Briedehoff's face was enough to prove it.

Ed said meagerly, "We can't leave Swan's woman over there."

"Maybe Mellish let Swan go."

"There was five shots," Ed said briefly, conclusively. He put his horse up the ridge, and they traveled that same trail that Ed and Pete had taken before.

The shack was still a heap of glowing coal. Crossing the valley, Ed swerved to haze over a freed horse which stood alertly, watching the dying fire over his shoulder. The horse and two riders headed for the shack.

Mrs. Ullman was still sitting on the ground, her sobs hard and tight and endless. She saw Ed and Steve without recognizing them, and Ed lifted her to her feet. "Where is Swan?" he asked, and she pointed to the hot coals.

"You better come along," Ed said gently to that despairing woman. "The rest of it is for us to do."

He took his rope and fashioned a hackamore for the loose mare, and the three of them took the road down to

Leston's. Mrs. Ullman never stopped crying. She made no effort to guide her horse, so that Ed, riding up beside her, put a hand on her horse's bridle and rode that way.

At Leston's Miles's wife took Mrs. Ullman into the house, and Ed briefly told Miles what had happened. Miles wanted to ride into Ten Troughs then, but Ed would not hear of it, and soon he and Steve left.

It was a wearing ride for Steve, who felt himself tired and yet savagely primed for a trouble that could not be fought now. Ed rode with the dogged deliberation of a range-bred man who knows the time is coming and who has the patience to wait for it. He did not hurry to Ten Troughs, and neither did he loiter. They got in at dawn and stabled their horses and ate a leisurely breakfast in a silence so deep that to an observer they would have appeared strangers.

Nance went into his office just as they were finishing their after-breakfast cigarettes, and Ed rose without a word to Steve and crossed to the office.

Nance's amiable reserved greeting died on his lips as he saw them.

"Swan got it," Ed said briefly. "They burned him out, too. They burned me out likewise."

"Ben?"

"Who else?"

Nance hunkered down in his chair and pulled out a drawer and absently shut it, face musing.

Ed said, "Nance, maybe I know how you feel about this, but it's no time to care much. I'm just tellin' you. Today I make the rounds of these men who won't belong to our association—our little bunch of penny-ante wise men. If I have any luck with them, Ben Mellish will lose half his riders within a week. He'll lose most of his cattle. His place will be burned and he'll be dead. And, by God, if you aim to stop me, I'll include you in on our Mutual Bushwhack Society, too. What about it?"

"Get some sleep," Nance said gently.

Ed replied mildly. "That's an idea, too." He turned to Steve and smiled sourly. "Did I ever claim our friend Pete

was a rash man? If I did, I was wrong, but maybe it ain't
too late to fix that. I'm goin' to get some sleep over at the
Legal Tender. Are you?"

"No."

"Ed, you sleep till I get back from the Anchor, I'll know
better what to do then. So will you," Nance said.

"I already know," Ed said, and left. Steve took the only
other chair and slumped into it, put elbows on knees, and
rubbed both palms over his face.

Nance, watching him, said, "I wouldn't make a move
for a while yet."

Steve stood up and walked to the door. "Don't talk to
me," he murmured. "Ed spoke his piece for me, too."

At the Legal Tender, Steve saw Ed stretched out on the
lone pool table in the rear, dead to the world. The bartender gave Steve his whisky, but it didn't do any good.
He was weary and sick inside him, but sleep was out of the
question. Cuddling the shot glass in his half-clenched
palm, Steve thought bitterly of his parting with Pete. If
only Pete had waited for Steve to tell him he was sorry, and
that he had spoken in a moment of discouragement. But
he hadn't, and right now, wherever Pete was, he was thinking of Steve as a quitter. It didn't matter that after Pete
had left, Steve had shamed and bullied and cajoled Ed
Briedehoff and Miles Leston into taking the offensive
again, and in trying again to round up these north Basin
ranchers on the morrow for a raiding party. It had come
too late; while they were waiting for tomorrow Ben Mellish had struck. And forever more Pete would think Ben
Mellish had crowded them into it, and that they had lacked
both the courage and foresight—and above all the leader-
ship—to take things in their own hands.

Nance left town and rode straight to the Anchor. He
had ample time to consider what he would do, so that
when he rode into the Anchor yard and dismounted before the bunkhouse, under the eyes of Blake and Ben Mellish and a half-dozen riders squatted in the shade of the
building, he didn't waste time.

"Better come along and face it now, Ben," Nance said, walking over to him. Ben and Blake lounged in the wide door. Ben's face wore an expression of heavy, obvious surprise, and he looked briefly at Blake, as if asking information.

"Come along where?" he said then.

"Town. It'll save the county money and me the trouble of deputizin' the town to come up and take you."

Ben whistled in low exclamation. "Wait a minute," he drawled. "What charges? Why deputies? What about this?"

Nance faced him, and he was standing on the ground so that he had to tilt his head back to see the face of Ben, who was standing on the log sill. It made him feel foolish, a little silly, and considerably at a disadvantage.

But he said stubbornly, "Killin' Swan Ullman and burnin' Briedehoff out. I haven't checked up on this yet, but I've got eyewitnesses."

Ben smiled broadly. "Let's get to the proof. What is it?"

"Two witnesses."

"It won't do," Ben murmured. "I was here all night. I've got a dozen men to prove it."

"I'll give them that chance at the hearing. Come along."

Blake shifted faintly in the doorway. His face was still swollen and marked with the blows Pete had given him, and his eyes, almost puffed shut, were vicious and calculating.

Ben said, "And let that bunch of nesters breed a lynch mob? What kind of a fool do I look like, Nance?"

"You won't come, then?"

"Hell, no," Ben drawled.

"I'll have to take you," Nance murmured, starting to raise his hand to his gun.

Blake, smiling evilly, kicked out savagely with his booted foot, and the blow caught Nance along the shelf of his jaw, sending him over backward into the dust. Blake, gun still in holster, walked over to him and flipped out Nance's gun and stood there while Nance, retching with the nausea of pain, rested on all fours for a moment and then rose unsteadily to his feet. He heard a man laugh.

"Stay away, Sheriff," Blake murmured.

Nance mounted and rode off without another word. Once out of sight of the house he reined up and got off his horse and retched again, and then felt his jaw gingerly, his face gray, the light of murder in his eyes. He knew that bluff about deputizing the town would never work. A sheriff stayed in office only on the sufferance of the people who put him there, and townsmen would not join a fight when they could remain neutral. And it was out of the question for him to deputize the north Basin ranchers. As for picking up a crew of anonymous ranch hands, that would be folly, since no one willingly commits suicide. Still, bluff or no bluff, Nance hadn't expected to be kicked like a dog. Any man deserved the honor of being fought with a gun. Somewhere in the back of his mind Sheriff Ross Nance filed a pledge to his Maker. Blake would never leave this county alive.

At a little past four in the afternoon Ben named off eight of his riders, who saddled up and then gathered beside the bunkhouse while Ben gave his instructions to Blake. Blake was to stay here, with four men, the cook, and horse wrangler, in case Nance really did bring his posse, which was a remote possibility. Ben and the others would take up their jobs where they had left off last night, and he and his eight riders filed out and took the west road.

After full dark, six men, led by Ed Briedehoff and Steve, moved down off the ridge from which they had been watching the Anchor since late afternoon and dismounted in a little gut at the edge of the timber well behind the Anchor.

They clustered about Ed, whose squat and burly shape stood beneath Steve's gangling alertness.

"By my count, there's six left, maybe more," Ed said. Nobody said anything, because they had all counted along with Ed. But they waited to hear him out. "By the law books," Ed went on doggedly, "this will be murder. Does anyone want to back out now?"

"Before it's too late," someone said.

"Yes."

There were no takers. "If any of you gag at this," Ed said in parting, "just remember Swan. Remember behind that, if you can."

They already had their directions, and split into two groups of four. Ed and Steve were in the same group, and they struck off past the cinders of the hay sheds toward the house. There was still a faint flavor of raw smoke in the air to remind them. Gaining the corrals, Ed walked out beyond them to look at the bunkhouse. One guard lounged in the doorway of the bunkhouse. Across the hard-packed dirt his rough and bawdy voice reached out to Ed, who knew this guard was more interested in the inside of the bunkhouse than what might happen on the outside.

Ed came back and said, "Just one. He's yarnin' and in the face of that lamplight. He couldn't see ten feet. If we don't kick up a racket, we can move over where we want."

He led off then. Slowly, noiselessly, out of the darkness of the corral and across this barn lot, he led the others. The guard looked out into the night only once and saw nothing, and turned his attention back to the company of his fellows. The next time he looked, the four of them were hidden from his sight by the corner of the bunkhouse.

A square of light lay aslant from the window in the end of the shack. It threw into relief a patch of ragged weeds, but on either side of it the darkness was profound, and it was for this square Ed worked his way.

Standing on the far edge of it he could see into the room. Two men lounged at the long center table. On the far end Blake was engaged in a morose and silent game of solitaire. The other voices came from the bunks. Once a man moved up to look over Blake's shoulder and said something which Blake did not even seem to hear.

Ed made a motion, and Steve and Cass Ford moved past him to the front corner of the shack. Abel Tohill, Cass's single rider, took the other side of the square and moved up to the wall of the shack.

Ed waited until he knew he had allowed enough time for Leston and the others to reach the rear window of the bunkhouse.

Then Ed raised his rifle to his shoulder, and against that lighted square of the room his sights were easily visible. He exhaled his breath slowly and then swung his sights in line, and when they settled rock-steady on Blake's temple he fired.

Blake went out of sight. Cass and Steve rounded the corner in time to cut down on the guard, who was half-erect in the door now. Ed and Abel, at either side of the window, were pumping shots at an oblique angle into the room. The swell of a cross fire from Miles at the rear window joined in before one of Blake's men had the sense to shoot out the light. It was still then, and there was a thin, tortured whisper in the room. Suddenly a flame appeared and a tangle of blazing tumbleweeds was forced through Miles's window to drop its torch on the floor, and a blast of gunfire felt for its placers.

By this light Ed shot a man under the table, and then, as rifle was added to rifle at the back window, these slugs hunted out every corner of the bunkhouse, every bunk where anything moved, every hidden cranny of this room that was lighted for only a dozen long seconds.

When the fire died there was again silence, and Ed pulled his rifle from the window with a rough clatter and said loudly, "Let's look."

He rounded the corner and Steve and Cass came out of the night to join him. Not waiting for Miles and his men, Ed struck a match on the doorframe and stepped over two bodies into the room. The match died and he groped on the long table for the lamp, whose chimney was shattered. By its weaving and uncertain light they hunted six men here, two shrinking even in death into the shelter of the bunks. Blake lay at ease on his face. One lay under the table, gun in hand. One more piled on the body of the guard as he was shot trying to win freedom.

"Get that wall lamp," Ed said briefly. It had been un-lighted. Both lamps were broken on the floor and Ed touched a match to it and followed the others outside.

Patiently, but not looking at each other, they waited for it to take. When the flames had started to lick out of the window, Ed said, "Now for the house."

They had not walked fifteen yards toward the house when a rifleshot kicked up dust at their feet. It came from a window in the second story of the main building, and Ed, paused, watching the window while the flame pushed back the darkness, presently said, "That was a woman."

The next shot, a little closer, warned them to scatter, and they made for the shelter of the corrals.

Steve turned to Ed and said savagely, "I won't help burn a woman alive, Ed! I won't even let you do it!"

"That house is goin' to be burned," Ed said grimly.

"Then fire one of the wings and give her a chance to get out."

Ed thought a minute and said, "All right." He disappeared into the dark of the corrals. Presently, at the end of one of the wings, they saw a flame start, idle a while, then, by the time Ed returned, lazily rise into a log-fed fire. In a few moments, when it had enough headway to resist any attempt at putting it out, they turned away to their horses. Ed was the last to leave, and when he caught up with Steve he only said quietly, "I don't love a hired gunhand."

Sarah, the fat Ute cook, watched them go and then came down and observed the fire. At the corral she caught the first horse that would come to her and saddled it and rode over to the flaming wing. Her dark and slack face was unreadable as she waited until the roof caved in at the far end of the wing. Then she went over and looped her rope around the end of a log against the main building and yet untouched by the flames. Mounting the pony, she dallied to the saddle horn and set him into the pull, and the log, free of the weight of the roof, came out abruptly, letting the others pile down on it. Its one end in flames, she dragged it off away from the house and went back for another. In half an hour she had the logs of this room strewn in a neat pile away from the house where they could harmlessly burn themselves out. She turned the horse loose then, her duty done, and went into the main house. The fire at the bunkhouse did not interest her, for these men were dead and had deserved their death.

And thus the Ten Troughs war swung into full stride. That night Ben Mellish burned four places, and not until he returned home did he think it strange that he had met with no resistance. Then he understood. Sarah, after telling him of the raid, made breakfast for the men, and it was served on the porch. Ben ate with his eight men, and his anger was smoldering and savage.

Halfway through the meal one of the men coughed and pitched forward onto his plate, and then the faint slap of a gunshot came through the still morning air. The men scrambled wildly for the door to the house. Balefully Ben regarded the edge of the timber below, from which the shot had come, then he, too, went inside.

After breakfast was finished and the men scattered to sleep, Ben saw two of them slip out and get their horses and ride off. He did not attempt to stop them. At noon one of his line riders who had been helping hold the Anchor herds far up in the mountains rode into the place with his hands wrapped across his middle and had to be helped off his horse. Before he fainted he told Ben that two of his riders were ambushed, the herd stampeded.

In late afternoon Ben saw a column of smoke rising over the pines far, far up the slope. He knew this would be the Burnt Creek line shack.

He roused two of his riders who were sleeping on the floor of the main room and told them to saddle up.

"Cut for their sign, and when you find it, stick to it. And when you find them, shoot them," he told them briefly. He watched them saddle up and take the trail up the slope, then he went over and looked again at the ashes of the bunkhouse. This couldn't go on, he thought darkly; a fight can't be won unless you carry it to the other fellow. Tonight he would take the rest of his men and cut a swath in this Basin that would settle this. He would take his fight to town; he would hire a hundred men if he had to.

Over at the corral he climbed the poles and sat atop it sunk in bitter thought. Ames Manderfield had not shown up yet, and there had been no word from him. It began to look as if what Pete Yard had said was true. Waranrode had withdrawn his help. It seemed that—

Ben raised his head, hearing a scattering of gunfire. He listened a long moment for more of it, trying to locate it. It came from up the slope. Maybe his boys had surprised the raiders. Climbing off the corral poles he walked toward the house. Halfway there he turned sharply to listen to the sound of running horses riding down the faint upland breeze. In another moment two ponies broke from the timber and trotted into the yard, their saddles empty. They were horses belonging to two riders he had sent up the slope not ten minutes ago.

That evening, as Ben lighted the big lamp and held it high to put in a bracket on the wall of the big room, it was shot out of his hand. The shot came through one of the rear windows. He stood there in the darkness, breathing hard, listening to the men crawl for shelter; and for the first time it came to him that he had started something that was now out of hand.

They munched biscuits in a dark house, and Ben sat in a deep chair, taking stock. His three men moved across the windows, not wanting to go outside, expecting more shots, which might come any time now. And Ben, watching them contemptuously, began to understand the shape of defeat.

CHAPTER SIXTEEN

IT IS NOT PLEASANT to watch fear take hold of a man, and Pete, over leveled gun, waited for it to wash Lassiter's face into drawn and loose misery. But it didn't. Lassiter raised his hands, his face still and cast into wariness. Pete stepped around the fire and took his gun and backed off, cocking the gun loudly in this still cage of firelit night.

Lassiter said tentatively, "You're doin' this for money?"

"Five hundred dollars."

Lassiter regarded him with speculative contempt, his glance falling to the guns and rising to Pete again. "The gov'ment is offerin' fifteen hundred for Linkman's killer."

"When this is over, I'll get that, too," Pete murmured. "You're it."

Lassiter shook his head slowly, not wanting to look at the guns now. "Maybe so. But if you collect it off me, you'll split it three ways. You, Nance, and Burke."

Pete nosed up his guns. "You've talked enough."

"I can tell you the murderer," Lassiter said calmly, and added with biting contempt, "As long as you're in it for money, get all you can. This won't be a split."

"Don't crawl."

"I can name you the man. It isn't me."

Pete pretended to consider this, and Lassiter saw his careful scowl. Quickly Lassiter said, "I'm goin' to put my hands down and then sit down. You just listen." He sat down as Pete carefully backed around to the side of him and squatted on his haunches.

Lassiter began to speak then in a measured, dry voice, his eyes shuttling keenly between Pete's face and the two leveled guns.

"You can see for yourself from what you've told me that Senator Waranrode is aimin' to hang this bushwhack on me. His riders found my horse; his riders brought in the two Utes who saw me. And he bribed you to get me off alone and put a bullet through my back. Is that all correct?"

Pete didn't answer, didn't move.

"Answer this, then. Why would Waranrode, a rich and respected man, want to get me out of the way?"

"I never even wondered," Pete answered coldly.

"Because I have somethin' on him, wouldn't you say?"

Pete shook his head slowly, and allowed himself a cynical smile. "No man who has anything on a man as rich as Waranrode is goin' to stay as poor as you are."

"How do you know I'm poor?" Lassiter countered.

"I saw your place."

"You didn't see my bank account," Lassiter said dryly. "It's well up in five figures. It's all banked in Cheyenne."

"What are you gettin' at?" Pete demanded impatiently. "Your money won't do you any good now."

"I'm tryin' to tell you I've been workin' for Waranrode, that he's paid me this money, that he's promised me more."

Pete said, with studied obtuseness, "What of it? So am I. What are you gettin' at?"

"I'm provin' to you that I've worked on a dirty job for Waranrode, and when you hear what the dirty job is you'll have your murderer and you can collect your reward."

"Who is it? Waranrode?" Pete demanded, showing some interest now.

Lassiter said patiently, as if he were addressing a child, "I want you to understand this. If you kill me you'll collect your money from Waranrode and maybe a third of the reward money. If you turn in the real murderer you'll collect more. You understand that?"

Pete cursed him for a fool in calculated, measured oaths. Lassiter heard him out, raised his hand bidding for silence.

"Sure, I'm a damn fool. But just listen. A year ago I sold my place, the Chevron, to Waranrode for thirty thousand dollars, twice what it was worth. He paid me another ten thousand to stay on the place and pretend it was mine."

Pete looked as if he didn't believe it.

Lassiter shifted to another tack. "You must have heard about the Ute reservation bein' cut down, didn't you? About part of it comin' up for public sale?"

"I heard it."

"The part that is comin' up for public sale ain't ten miles from here. Every foot of it joins Chevron range."

"What of it?"

"I've got instructions to bid on it at public sale—to bid and take half of it, and let Fonse Schumacher up north bid against me and get the other half. And both of us are buyin' it for Waranrode."

Pete said carefully, dubious, "You liar. It was only decided a week ago, and if they published what part was comin' up for sale, it hadn't reached Ten Troughs when I left."

Lassiter smiled in quiet triumph. "It was decided months ago—decided between Waranrode and Major Linkman, the Ute agent. Linkman drove the Utes into lettin' go that piece. And lucky for him it was the most useless piece on their range."

Pete felt excitement crawl through him, but he stared at Lassiter with remote and hard suspicion. Then he said slowly, "Old man, you're lyin'. It makes a good story—but it happens I've been over that piece of the reservation. You couldn't run fifteen hundred head of cattle on the whole thing, and to Waranrode fifteen hundred head isn't worth the drive to Wheeler."

"Who said anything about cattle?" Lassiter asked slowly. "There's coal there—hundreds of thousands of tons of it layin' under the surface for the man that's got eyes to see it."

Pete took a tight and savage grip on his guns to steady them, and the breath caught in his chest and he rose, for the blood in him seemed racing too fast for stillness. But he said nothing.

"Linkman knew it and never reported it," Lassiter went on. "He's the one that come to Waranrode with the scheme to get it out of government hands and Waranrode pulled the strings in Washington. Him and Linkman were to split it."

Pete said gently, skeptically, "And what?"

"So Waranrode had Linkman murdered."

"The proof."

And now Lassiter allowed himself a smile. "Two days before the Ute chiefs met, Linkman rode over to my place. He wanted me to double-cross Waranrode. His idea was when I bid and got half the land, I was to deed him my half for one hundred thousand dollars cash."

Pete licked his lips. "And you did it?"

"I told him I would. But when he was gone I rode over to Waranrode and told him Linkman's proposition." He paused. "Waranrode killed him. Who else could?" He hesitated, watching belief take hold in Pete's face, for it was a belief that Pete could not hide. Here, beyond the faintest doubt, was the whole story, enough to hang Waranrode.

Lassiter was saying, "Waranrode is panicked. Before Linkman told me the whole story I couldn't have hurt Waranrode. Now I can." His voice was merciless. "And if you'll wait, I will."

Pete rose and walked around the fire, his guns hanging at his sides.

Lassiter murmured, "The whole reward is yours. I won't claim a cent. Do you believe me?"

Pete looked up swiftly. "Will you tell that to an army man? And tell him the reward money is mine?"

Lassiter nodded.

Pete pulled out a handkerchief and wiped the sweat from his face. He took the rope from his saddle, because if he was working he could hide his trembling excitement from Lassiter. Later, when Lassiter lay trussed by the fire, and Pete went out to catch up the horses, he settled himself into the old calm again, so that when he returned with the horses his eyes showed Lassiter only the greed he pretended.

With Lassiter's legs roped under the belly of his horse, Pete scattered the coals of the fire and they rode off toward the reservation.

They rode all that night and far into the next day, so that it was late afternoon when they swung through the Ute camp for the dogs to bark at and the children to stare at. Pete sat his saddle heavily, aware that in these next few minutes he would have to have all his wits about him, and yet this weariness rode him with an iron hand. He had crowded his luck this far, played his bluff with a hard shrewdness, but it was not finished yet. He would have to find the investigating officer sent by the army and convince him that, before any questions were asked of Lassiter, this weary and disillusioned man must be allowed to talk and to talk freely. On that depended his whole scheme, for once Lassiter learned through being questioned that no black horse had been found, that he was not even suspected, that Pete had played a bitter hoax on him, he would not talk. And without his talk Pete knew his case would be lost.

There were two cavalry regulars lounging under the wooden awning of the trader's store as they passed, and Pete's hopes rose, for it indicated that he had guessed rightly in thinking the army investigator would have arrived by now.

He glanced obliquely at Lassiter, who was as weary as himself. A look of apathy was clouding his eyes, and he regarded the army men with no surprise, only an indifference that heartened Pete.

They rode on up to the agency residence and Pete saw a cluster of Utes squatting in the shade of the office. Two soldiers stood at ease on either side of the open doorway.

Pete swung off at the hitchrack and took Lassiter's reins and tied his pony, while the soldiers observed him with awakening curiosity. Saddle-stiff and weary, he walked to them, and one observed, "Can't go in, fella. Colonel Knight's at work."

Pete said, "Tell him I've got some information about the murder of Linkman."

The soldier looked dubious and jerked his head toward Lassiter. "I suppose that's the puncher that shot him."

"See what the colonel thinks." Pete grinned. The soldier looked hard at him and then went inside. Pete could hear him talking to another man, and soon he returned and said, "He'll see you."

Pete entered the small room to find a man in army blue seated in the lone easy chair beside a desk, at which another army man sat taking notes. Two Utes, one an interpreter, stood before the colonel, and now he dismissed them and regarded Pete.

Pete's first impression of Colonel Knight was that of a

sensible and fair man harassed by fatigue and frustration. He was heavy, partially bald, with a sensitive, tired face. He said courteously, "What is it, my man?"

Pete said gently, "You know how to listen, Colonel?"

Colonel Knight removed the cigar from his mouth and stared at Pete, frowning. Hours of examining most of the Ute Indians here had not improved his temper, but on the other hand, he was a man of some humor, and to be asked such a question appealed to his sense of irony, for he had done nothing but listen for three days. "I do," he said, still courteously, and added with a touch of faint sarcasm that was relieved by a smile, "I have practically memorized the Ute language by listening to it. Does this concern Major Linkman's death?"

"It does. I want another favor besides."

"What is that?"

Pete indicated the man at the desk. "Is he your secretary?"

"Adjutant."

"Tell him to get a clean sheet and take this down. I'm bringin' a man in here. Don't ask him his name. Don't ask him a question until he's through talkin'. Just listen—and write down what he says. Will you do it?"

The colonel leaned forward and said, "Certainly. What man?"

"Shall I get him?"

"By all means."

Pete went out and untied Lassiter and followed him into the room. Pete said, "Lassiter, this is Colonel Knight. Take a chair and tell him what you told me."

Colonel Knight offered Lassiter his own chair, which was accepted; and he shot a questioning glance at Pete, which Pete ignored.

"Start from the beginning, when you sold your place," Pete said.

In a flat monotone Lassiter launched into his story. It was complete, and he outlined enough of it for Colonel Knight to understand the background. At the tenth mention of Senator Waranrode, Knight looked over at Pete, who shook his head faintly. Starting with the purchase of the Chevron, Lassiter progressed to the murder, to Pete's call, to Pete's threat, to the confession of Linkman's visit to him, and to the conclusions which he voiced very simply. "There's only one man that could have killed Linkman, Colonel. That man is Waranrode. As for that black horse that was stolen from my range and left as evidence against me, I leave it to you to figure out who planted it, and who framed the evidence."

The adjutant had ceased writing, and now he sat back in his chair and massaged his pen hand. Colonel Knight, a look of frank amazement on his face, said, "Yes, that horse. What about him? You've mentioned that several times."

"That horse," Pete murmured, "was an idea of my own. I caught him up on Lassiter's range and used him to blackmail the story out of Lassiter."

Lassiter turned bleak eyes on Pete, and his face flushed. "You ain't a deputy? That horse—it—you never—"

"Corporal!" the colonel called, and one of the soldiers stepped inside. "Both you men take this man into Mrs. Linkman's parlor and guard him."

Lassiter's protest was over, and he seemed to be more relieved that his secret was out than angry with Pete's ways. He rose wearily and marched ahead of them. Colonel Knight did not even watch him go. He came over and stood before Pete and said, "Who is he? Tell me how you got him. Tell me who you are."

Pete told his side of it then, and in the telling he brought in the Ten Troughs war, Ben Mellish, Steve and his kidnaping—all of it, from his own earliest days with the G.W. through his bluff to Lassiter. And Colonel Knight kept his eyes on Pete's face, and the adjutant wrote swiftly and interminably. When Pete had finished, Colonel Knight sat down and stared out the open doorway. He put a cigar in his mouth and promptly forgot to light it. Several times he got ready to speak, and then didn't. Finally, he rose and stood in the doorway, and then turned to Pete.

"Yard, I don't think you realize what you've laid before me. Waranrode is a public figure and—and I just can't believe it."

"I worked for him for three years, and I would have shot the man hinting at a story like this," Pete said.

"I want to be fair," Colonel Knight continued. "I'll have to check your record. I'll have to take into custody for questioning Lassiter's cook, who saw Linkman at the Chevron, your Steve Trueblood, and Schumacher. I'll have to get to a telegraph to wire Cheyenne and verify Lassiter's bank account. I'll have to question the Ute chiefs again. Every step I take will have to be checked and rechecked."

Pete rose and took Colonel Knight's arm and turned him around, pointing to the chair. "Sit down, Colonel." Colonel Knight did. Pete faced him, his body high and wide and stubborn. "How long have you been in the West here, Colonel?"

"Seven months."

"I've been here all my life," Pete murmured. "Let me tell you where you're wrong. You send two men over to pick up that cook and Schumacher. Before your troopers have picked up Lassiter's cook, Schumacher will be dead. More than that, there's not one chance in five hundred that your cook will arrive here alive. There's even less chance that Jim Lassiter will live a week. There's no chance at all that Steve Trueblood will be allowed to live to tell you anything. As for myself, I would take to the brush and travel day and night to put seven ranges of mountains between me and Senator Waranrode." Paused, he smiled and shook his head slowly. "You see, in the East, when a man like Waranrode is accused of this crime, he hires the best lawyers in the country. Here a man sees to it that he isn't accused. That's the difference."

"You mean he'd kill all these men who could testify against him?"

"He would."

Colonel Knight looked hard at Pete. "Then what am I to do—supposing what you say is true?"

"You don't have to suppose it," Pete said. "Look what happened to Linkman."

"All right, but what am I to do?"

Pete said quickly, "There's a Ute subchief here in camp. His name is Stumbling Bear. He knows this country like you know the parts of a gun, and he is honest. If you've got a trooper here you can trust, and who isn't prejudiced against an Indian, take the uniform off him and tell him to obey every order Stumbling Bear gives him. Put Lassiter in the care of those two men and forget him, and when you need him to testify, he'll be brought in alive."

"But he'll be safe in jail!"

"Every jail has got a window," Pete said. "And no window is so small a rifle bullet won't go through it."

Colonel Knight considered this with impassive face. "All right. What next?"

"Your commission gives you the authority to place under military arrest anyone suspected of the murder of Major Linkman, or anyone concerned with the murder, doesn't it?"

"In effect, yes."

Pete said calmly, "Go over and arrest Waranrode and hold him, and don't let a single man talk to him without an army order."

Knight looked up at him swiftly. "But the evidence."

"Evidence be damned!" Pete said harshly. "Get the evidence after you've got him bottled and corked, or you'll never get it at all!"

Colonel Knight rose and paced the room. Suddenly he stopped and said to Pete, "In other words, it's up to him to prove his innocence. It's not up to me to prove his guilt."

"That's pretty close."

"All American law is founded on the supposition that a man is innocent till proved guilty. It's his right."

"Does it say anything about the rights of a curly wolf?" Pete murmured.

Knight frowned grimly. "Of course, you know I'd be

broken—possibly cashiered—if this was a mistake."

"And you'd be made a major general if it wasn't."

Pete waited until Colonel Knight sat down again and pressed his palms together and scowled at the floor. Pete knew the army habit of mind well enough to know that what he was suggesting was contrary to its way. But he also knew the army had a custom of rewarding men who knew when to overstep their authority. And he thought he knew Knight.

He said quietly, "You took an oath once, Colonel. And in livin' up to it you've fought Kiowas and Sioux and Comanches and Apaches. But you'll never have the chance again to protect your people against a worse kind of savage—the kind Waranrode is."

Colonel Knight put both hands on the arms of his chair and rose, facing Pete. "When my superior officer sent me on this job he told me to be sure and do one thing—look up Doctor Benbow, an old army surgeon friend of his who was cashiered for drinking, but who was the wisest, most honest man he had ever known. I looked up Doctor Benbow the night I got in on the Ten Troughs stage." He smiled a little now. "Do you know the only advice he gave me? It was to hunt down Pete Yard and hire him, and once I hired him, to believe in him." He turned away. "I think I'll do it."

He drew up a chair beside his adjutant and motioned to it. "Sit down. Tell my adjutant the entire story—putting in the proof where you have it, and leaving it out when you don't. When you're finished we'll hunt up your Stumbling Bear and turn Lassiter over to him. And when that's done I'll ride over to the G.W.—but not to collect that dinner Senator Waranrode invited me to."

CHAPTER SEVENTEEN

AMES WAS TOLD to take his time with the job, and to do it well, so the first three days he was in Ten Troughs he kept to the saloons and listened. Nowadays Ten Troughs was not a curious town, so that he was never questioned, and by keeping his own counsel he learned of the progress of the war. He heard about the raid on the Anchor, and he smiled at his drink. It seemed that these Basin ranchers would relieve him of part of his job. Twice, idling in the dark in front of the Melodian, he saw Steve Trueblood ride into town in company with Ed Briedehoff and others. After they stabled their horses they would go into the Exchange House for the night.

Ames turned this fact over in his mind, tasting its possibilities. The chances were he could get away with it; but to find their room he would have to ask the clerk or find it himself, and either method entailed a little risk. So he waited.

And while he did, many things happened along that main street of Ten Troughs that did not escape him. Sylvia Waranrode was in town. Ames knew that Waranrode hated having Linkman murdered when Sylvia was visiting the agency, but at that time haste was imperative. And Sylvia had flatly disobeyed her father's orders to come home after it had happened. Instead she had come here to Ten Troughs to watch over Mrs. Linkman. Or did she? Ames wondered. How much of all this did she link with her father? Very little, Ames guessed, despite the fact that she talked often with Christina Mellish. The only men who knew Waranrode's part in this war were not the kind who would hurt a woman.

Another thing Ames had noticed was that Christina Mellish had left her hotel room for a tiny shack in the alley behind Doctor Benbow's. He had even passed it one night, purely out of curiosity. The night the army investigator got off the stage at Ten Troughs and went immediately to Doc Benbow's, Ames had a bad few moments. This move was unexpected, signifying something that Ames did not rightly understand. But by the next night it was gossiped around the saloons that the army man was an old friend of Doc's service days. Of course, Doc Benbow would know everything Steve Trueblood and Pete Yard knew, but that would never be tied in with Linkman's murder, and would apply only to this Ten Troughs war.

So Ames waited—in daytime inside the saloons, at night in the dark shadows of the street. Word had reached town this afternoon that Ben Mellish and three of his riders had ridden into an ambush of the north Basin ranchers. Ben Mellish was hit, but not badly, and he had escaped. And Ames, who had studied the movements of Trueblood and his men, reckoned that Trueblood would come into Ten Troughs sometime tonight.

Ames kept to himself, avoiding the saloons and the passers-by when he could. He smoked a half-dozen cigarettes in the dark, set-back doorway of Pearson's Emporium, and then crossed the street to stand in the dark slit between two unlighted business buildings. During that hour and a half two riders left town and none entered. But Ames had patience, and he liked his place of concealment.

Presently, when most of the town's activity was concentrated at the two saloons, the feed corral, and the hotel, Ames heard some riders upstreet. There were five of them, and one was Steve Trueblood. Ames swung out of his hiding-place and turned the corner, and then ran for the alley that snaked behind the feed stable and corral. His rifle was where he left it after dark, against the side of the stable and inside the corral. He levered a shell in the chamber and then walked through the corral and softly swung the gate open. A week of watching this corral, day and night, had taught him the routine of the place, and this did not include a lantern in the rear at night. As he stood in the gate opening he heard the soft padding of the penned horses as they approached him, eager for any chance to leave the corral. From here he could look straight through the long centerway of the stable, at the head of which the lantern hung from a nail.

Even as he was watching, five horsemen swung into the arch and dismounted, their forms silhouetted against the light of the street. Ames had no trouble picking out Steve, who stood beside his horse talking to the stable boy.

It was difficult for Ames to sight his gun, and almost slacking it off he decided to wait. But when Steve turned to unsaddle, broadside to him, Ames could not resist. He raised his gun again and fired, and saw Steve go down.

The horses behind him snorted. Casually, almost, Ames stepped away from the gate and the horses trotted through. The last one Ames kicked viciously in the belly, and it stampeded into the others, who stretched out in a run down the twisting alley.

Ames dropped his gun and walked back across the corral, climbed the fence, and listened a minute. The ranchers' horses in the centerway were out of control, and Ames could hear the thunder of their hoofs on the plank floor mingled with the shouting of the men.

When the first man raced out beside the corral and yelled and pointed up the alley, Ames allowed himself a meager smile. He traveled the narrow littered way between two buildings and approached the sidewalk cautiously. He smiled again now, for his wait had allowed the loafers on the hotel porch to leave their chairs and run for the stable. Momentarily the sidewalks were cleared of people who had collected at the stable. Ames sidled out and turned down toward the stable and stopped there in the growing knot of watchers. He waited until Steve had been picked up and carried off toward Doctor Benbow's, and then he asked a neighbor, "Dead?"

"I dunno. Them Anchor hands are usually good shots."

Ames drifted across the street and into the hotel and inquired after the number of Sylvia's room. At the end of the first-floor corridor he noticed the window was open, and a fresh breeze whipped out the curtains.

Sylvia opened to his knock, and her greeting was indifferent, almost hostile, and Ames smiled slightly and took off his hat.

"I know. Dad wants me to come home, doesn't he?" Sylvia asked bluntly.

"That's about it," Ames said, his lean face watchful and grave now. "He's worried."

"Didn't he know I was here with Mrs. Linkman?"

"Yes, but this is no safe place for a woman now. He says to come home."

Sylvia shook her head and smiled. "Sorry, Ames, but I'm of age now. I'll be home when it pleases me."

Ames shrugged. "It's up to you. There's no one to nurse him but Mrs. Sais."

Sylvia said swiftly, "He's sick?" and Ames nodded.

Sylvia looked at him a long time, and he held her gaze. Finally, she smiled. "I've lived with you too long, Ames. You're a liar. Good night."

Ames said, "Good night," and went out. Outside her door he paused and drew out a sack of tobacco. He was sifting out the tobacco onto the paper when the whole corridor exploded with sound, but before even a noise could register with Ames, something drove into his back and blossomed out his chest in a hell of pain and he fell, his own blood pooling beneath him and creeping out of the corner of his mouth in a slow, strangling trickle.

Softly Ben Mellish closed the door of the linen closet in which he had been hiding, and sank down on the linen, cuddling his warm gun in his hand, his head hung low on his chest. Beyond that wire-taut sickness that passed wave on wave through his body he felt something like satisfaction. If he was licked, then it was not Ames Manderfield who did it. He felt the blood on his boot cold to his foot, and every time he moved something warm again flushed his thigh. It angered him that he should be so weak, and from beneath him he pulled out a cloth and wrapped it tightly around his leg—and listened, hearing the first tentative movements of someone in the corridor. Then a woman's scream, shriek after shriek, sounded in the corridor, and again Ben's head sunk on his chest, and he waited.

At first dark he had ridden into town, hunkered down in his saddle, stuck to it by his own dried blood. This morning he and his three remaining men—all that were left him—had been ambushed at Cass Ford's house when they rode up to burn it. Ben had a vague and savage mem-

ory of a fight, and of riding away, his leg a bloody, aching
pulp where the blast of a shotgun had channeled it as he
wheeled his horse away from the door of Ford's house.
Later, miles away from it, he had pulled up in that hot
morning sunshine that was already sickening him, and
read his own future. Unless he could hide, he would die.
And this morning he had not a friend, not a hired gunman, not a man or woman to turn to in his need. He was
beaten and sick and afraid to die. Then he thought of
Chris, and with the blind and unquestioning faith of a
child he knew she would take care of him and hide him
if he could only get to her. He had left her in her room on
the first floor of the Exchange House, and he returned
there to find her. By what processes of torture he could
not remember, he had climbed the sheds to the roofs and
from the roofs he had got in that back hotel-corridor window, which he did not even try to close. But Chris's room
door was locked, and he had not the strength to crash the
lock. So he hid in this linen closet, waiting for her, bleeding slowly and irrevocably his own hot blood. The sound
of Ames closing Sylvia's door had roused him, and when
he inched open his own door to see Ames's broad back the
memory of that glove and of Pete Yard's cold and knowing
advice came to him. He had killed him, thinking that if
he was licked, it was not Ames Manderfield who had done
it.

And now he heard the gathering commotion in the hall,
and he waited for this door to open. Discovery would be
blessed and welcome. But it never came, and as Ben listened to the activity outside his door he remembered the
open window. They would think the murderer escaped.

Well after the commotion had died, Ben rose and stumbled out. Slowly he made his way down to Chris's old
room. Again it was locked, and again he did not have the
strength to open it. With that knowledge came a tenfold
terror of dying. He *had* to find her, he *had* to have her
help. And suddenly he thought of Doctor Benbow, and he
turned to look down the corridor. Doc Benbow would
help him in spite of what he had done to Doc. If he could

make Doc Benbow's he would be saved.

This time the rope fire escape coiled on its hook by the window pointed a merciful way to him. In the dark alley below he reeled and stumbled, clinging to the sheds for support, heading up the alley toward Doc's.

The street would be the hardest to cross, but he walked out into it with indomitable strength. Three quarters of the way across it he knew he was going to fall, and he tried to run. He made the mouth of the alley and its shadow before he pitched on his face in the cinders.

Lying there against the back of Pearson's Emporium, barely conscious, he saw three men leave Doc Benbow's. But they were Ed Briedehoff and Miles Leston and Cass Ford, and if they found him they would shoot him. He did not call, letting them go.

He lay there, waiting, terror coiling his entrails. If he was to shout, there was the chance that another Basin rancher would come out of Doc's. While he was lying there, his mind almost made up to shout, the door opened and Chris stepped out and turned up the alley.

Ben called to her, and Chris stopped and turned and slowly retraced her steps. And then she saw him and ran to him.

"Hide me," Ben whispered. "I'm hurt! But you've got to hide me!"

"I'll get Doctor—"

"No! No! Hide me," Ben pleaded, for now that he had her he did not care about Doc Benbow. All he wanted was the security she could give him.

She managed to get him on his feet, and slinging his arm across her shoulder she moved down the dark alley. Ben wanted to ask where she was going, but he was too tired.

Chris got the door to her shack open and hauled Ben inside and laid him on the bed, then shut the door and pulled the curtains to and struck a light.

One whole side of him was matted with blood, and his face was pale and drawn. When he opened his eyes they were tortured with fright. In that moment Chris forgot all her hatred for him and remembered only that this was her brother, and that he might die.

At her touch Ben opened his eyes and took her hand and clung to it.

"I'll be all right," he murmured. "Only hide me, Chris—for old times' sake! Hide me and don't let them at me!"

Chris only nodded mutely.

CHAPTER EIGHTEEN

WHEN THE G.W. WAS IN SIGHT across the green prairie, Colonel Knight raised a hand and reined up. Pete pulled his horse in, and the six troopers and the adjutant behind stopped, too. Colonel Knight was dressed in neat blue, and sat his horse with a ramrod-straight seat. His carriage was strictly military, even to the cast of his face, which was less sensitive and more determined than Pete had ever seen it.

"You stay here in the timber, Pete," the colonel said.

"I don't like to leave a thing half finished," Pete drawled. "I started this and—"

"The army will end it. No, I'm not taking a chance. I can handle it better alone."

"But he'll see me when you bring him back."

"Well and good. That's time enough." He raised a hand and spurred his horse on, and the troopers filed past Pete until they were abreast their colonel.

Colonel Knight approached the G.W. at a leisurely pace and with a reluctance which was almost a physical thing, for he was far from a long-shot gambler. The next few minutes would decide his whole future in the army. But he was also a man of convictions who understood well the spirit behind duty and discipline, and his conscience was easy. Nevertheless he wished with bitter impotence that Waranrode had not sent his man over to the reservation that first day with a note of welcome which pledged his support and at the same time invited the colonel to be a guest of the G.W. at the earliest opportunity.

The sight of the place did not help Colonel Knight any. No one had told him how grand and imposing it was, nor of its beauty, nor of its air of incorruptible wealth and good taste. He took the main road into the place, which skirted the plaza and led straight to the giant cottonwoods and water.

With sinking heart, Knight saw that Waranrode was standing on the long porch, and that he waved as Knight and his men rode into the yard.

Dismounting, Knight said to his adjutant, "Craig, come along. Sergeant, dismount and be ready for Craig's orders from the house." Then Colonel Knight stepped away from Craig and walked over to meet Waranrode, who stood at the gate.

He saluted and took Waranrode's hand, but his face was unsmiling as he listened to the senator say, "Well, I was afraid I'd have to do without you a few days more, Colonel Knight—which makes this surprise twice as welcome."

Knight bowed stiffly and said, "Senator Waranrode, I don't wish to trade on your hospitality. I have come on a far more important errand than enjoying your dinner."

A flicker of caution crossed Waranrode's eyes, but he was too able at dealing with men to betray it any other way. He smiled. "Errand, you say? Out with it."

"I have come to place you under military arrest and to conduct you to the reservation."

Not a sign of anything but polite disbelief showed on Waranrode's face. "Arrest. That's interesting. I dare say you can explain it as well in a chair as you can here. Come along."

He led the way to the porch and indicated a seat, and when Knight declined he sat down himself. "Let's hear it."

Colonel Knight said briefly, "It is my duty to arrest you as accessory to the murder of Major Linkman."

After a moment's pause Waranrode observed dryly, "That's interesting, especially in view of the fact that he was one of my oldest and dearest friends."

Knight reached inside his tunic and drew out a thick sheaf of folded paper. "Perhaps this will tell you more than I can, Senator Waranrode."

Waranrode accepted the paper and looked at it without opening it. "What is this?"

"Proof that you were in league with Major Linkman to defraud the government out of considerable property. But that is only incidental. The immediate charge is the one I've already named."

Waranrode smiled absently and nodded and laid the papers in his lap. "Would you care for a drink, Colonel Knight? A cigar?"

"Neither, thanks."

Waranrode rose. "Then if you'll excuse me, I'll take these up to my study and look them over. They are bound to be important, I assure you, especially"—and here his voice carried an undertone of pointed sarcasm—"to my army friends."

Again Colonel Knight bowed, and Waranrode left. He did not hurry up the stairs, and once he was seated in his study he lighted a cigar before he took up the papers, broke the seal, and read. At the top of the first page was the notation: *Copy, original filed with Commandant at Fort Kiowa.* He read on. It was written in the quiet form of an indictment, with the personal pronoun *you* introducing nearly every paragraph.

As he continued, Senator Waranrode removed the cigar from his mouth and laid it on the table without looking where he put it. The clock on the wall ticked loudly in the room, its only contender against utter silence the occasional rustle of paper when he leafed over a page. When he was finished he let his hand holding the paper sink gently into his lap.

Yes, that covered it all. Except for a few minor inaccuracies, it was complete. The reason for his wanting the coal, of course, was not mentioned, but then, this had always been a secret between himself and Senator Crippen of Delaware and Ames Manderfield. Immediately his mind flicked back to the source of this information. Without a doubt it was Jim Lassiter. Which argued that Lassiter was in the hands of the army now. Schumacher was or soon would be. Trueblood and Yard had doubtless given Knight the information. Mellish was dead by now, but a determined Congressional committee could soon ferret out Waranrode's connection with him.

Heedless of the cigar burning beside him, he drew out a fresh one and lighted it and settled down in the chair. Colonel Knight had said arrest, which meant that he would be escorted back to the reservation and jailed. If Ames were here now—this minute, this second—there would be a possibility of avoiding this charge by doing away with the witnesses, but Ames was not here. And Colonel Knight was downstairs waiting.

Carefully Waranrode weighed his chances of fighting this charge and winning. With the best lawyers, with some luck at bribing, with more luck at getting at the witnesses, it might be done. But Knight, with full authority, would keep him incommunicado until all witnesses were safe. The bulk of the evidence was inferential, but the sum of it was great, and what was worse, correct. Even if he fought the charge and beat it, he was certain to be impeached by the Senate. Moreover, his plan to purchase the Ute lands was overboard now, destroyed by this publicity.

Supposing he was freed and later impeached, he would come out of it an old man, dishonored in life and office, cursed by a rabble he always believed he could persuade into liking him. Waranrode was an honest man with himself, and he did not even bother to try and convince himself that life would still be bearable in the face of all this. He knew it wouldn't. It would be hell until he died, and even his death would be unhonored.

Looking back with a surprising calm, he could see where he had made his mistakes. Although this document did not say so, he knew Steve Trueblood and Pete Yard were responsible for the uncovering of its material. Therein lay his mistake. His plan—to promote this Ten Troughs war as a means of anonymously killing Steve Trueblood, and as a screen for his steal—had been admirable. But he had waited too long. A wiser man than himself would have put those two out of the way in the very beginning. He had made the serious error of not crediting them with an intelligence equal to his own—or even to Ames's. In an impersonal way he admired them.

He thought briefly of Sylvia. She was grown, she would have money—and money, he still believed, counted more than anything else. He doubted if she would miss him, certainly not if she learned everything about him. That was inescapable.

Turning to his desk he dipped his pen in ink and read over the document again. Occasionally he inserted a date in his fine, neat script; less often he made a correction. At the end, on the blank half-page, he wrote neatly, *Substantially correct. Matthew Waranrode.* He was about to lay his pen down when he paused, and added the line: *Colonel Knight. If it is possible and compatible with your conscience, and the conscience of your superiors, I ask that judgment against me be rendered in secret.*

He rose, folding the paper, and yanked the pull-rope by the door on his way across the room. At the wall safe he paused and turned the combination and swung the door open. Taking out a steel box, he opened it. It was crammed to the top with fresh bank notes, all yellowbacks. To be exact, there was a little less than seventy-five thousand dollars in all.

On his way to the desk he answered a knock on the door, and Mrs. Sais, the fat and comfortable Mexican housekeeper, stepped inside.

"One moment, Mrs. Sais," Waranrode said. "Be seated."

At his desk he drew out a clean sheet of notepaper and hesitated a moment before he wrote, *My dear Colonel Knight: If one of your couriers can overtake the mail and retrieve the original of this document, returning it to me, I will pledge myself to triple the amount contained herein.*

He wrapped the note and the money in a wide sheet of paper, rose, and handed it to Mrs. Sais, saying, "There is an army officer below on the porch, Mrs. Sais. Give him this and wait for an answer."

Mrs. Sais was gone only a little more than two minutes. When she returned she handed the package to Waranrode. "He asked me to return it to you with his regrets, sir," she said quietly.

"Thank you, Mrs. Sais. That is all."

Mrs. Sais let herself out and waddled down the corridor. Nearing the end of it, she was arrested by the sound of a gunshot. By the time she had hurried back down the corridor Colonel Knight appeared at the top of the stairs, and behind him was Adjutant Craig. Mrs. Sais said, "In there," and Knight opened the door.

Waranrode was seated limply in his customary chair, head slumped on chest. The gun was on the floor, where it had slacked from his hand.

Colonel Knight crossed over to him and looked at him with pity in his eyes.

"That," he said, maybe to Waranrode, maybe to Craig, maybe only to himself, "was the only way left."

CHAPTER NINETEEN

CHRIS DID NOT SHOW HER PANIC until Ben lapsed into unconsciousness, and then she looked at his leg. She did not know what to do. Like a trusting child, Ben assumed she could take care of him, and was quietly bleeding to death. She washed out the wound, and still the blood seeped out. In desperation, she applied the remedy of a pioneer people; she poured flour on the wound, trusting to its clean adhesiveness to clot the blood.

Then she considered. Ben was unconscious. He would never know if Doc Benbow looked at him or not; and, without thinking longer on it, Chris made her decision.

Doctor Benbow was alone with Steve Trueblood, who occupied the lone bedroom.

When he saw her, Doc said, "Ready to stay the night?"

"Will he live?"

"Probably. It isn't bad. I got the slug out without any trouble."

Chris announced swiftly, "Ben is in my place, Uncle Doc. He's hurt badly. Will you come look at him?"

Doc's private emotion at this news was one of satisfaction, but he only nodded and packed his black bag. On the way down the alley Chris told him of finding Ben, and of his plea to be hidden. When she was finished, Doc observed, "Ed Briedehoff tells me Ben has played out his hand. He hasn't a man left." He tried to see her face in the dark. "Ed says he knows Ben shot Trueblood. He says when they've hunted Ben out and killed him they'll hang up their guns, and not till then."

"Ben knows that, Uncle Doc."

"Good," Doc grunted. "He knew it before. Maybe he'll believe it now."

"You won't give him away?"

"I ought to," Doc said grimly, and added, "No, I won't."

Doc's first act was to give Ben an opiate hypodermic, and then he examined and dressed the wound. Finished, he said, "He'll never know I was here unless you tell him." He put on his coat and looked up at Chris and said, "If you're going to worry, don't. He was more scared than truthful. He can't be killed—more's the pity."

Chris didn't look at Doc then. She was watching Ben with a dispassionate curiosity, and it was hard for Doc to guess what was running through her mind. But his lip pouted in anger and he scrubbed his clipped head in an impatient gesture.

He said gruffly, "Chris, are you going to let him do this last thing to you, make you nurse him and hide him?"

"He's my brother."

"The Lord God himself wouldn't hold you to that!" Doc said in violent blasphemy. "Tomorrow Ben will be awake and plotting a bullheaded revenge, and when he can walk he'll try to carry it out. Why don't you let me talk to Nance? In a couple of days Nance can take him away in a spring wagon."

"Where?"

"Hell, what does it matter?" Doc said angrily. "Away from you. And once he's gone I'll put up a reward myself to keep him out of this country."

Chris only shook her head and smiled faintly, and Doc subsided.

"What am I going to do for a nurse for Trueblood?" he grumbled. "You won't leave Ben, I suppose?"

Again Chris shook her head. Then, remembering, she said, "You remember the girl, Sylvia Waranrode, who is attending Mrs. Linkman?"

"She's a senator's daughter," Doc said wryly.

"She'd help you if you need her," Chris said. "I'll go over and ask her."

So Sylvia, at Chris's request, spent her time at Steve Trueblood's bedside, and Chris watched after Ben. It took some reluctant scheming on Doc's part to keep Ben's hiding-place a secret. When Chris did not show up the next day, Sylvia wanted to go and see her, and it was then Doc told his first lie. "You won't go near her place," he said abruptly, and when Sylvia asked why, Doc said, "She's in bed. No, she's not sick, just worn out, and she's got a cold. If you go down there and visit her, you'll catch her cold and bring it back here. And once your patient gets the cold, I'll have a warrant out for you for murder. You stay here."

"But who will look after her?" Sylvia asked.

Doc said, "I see her three times a day and I take her meals to her. The rest of the time she sleeps."

To back that statement up, Doc had to carry a tray from his kitchen to Chris's shack three times a day and Chris had to stay penned up with Ben. Inevitably Ben learned that Doc shared the secret of his hiding-place, but he would never allow Doc to come in. And each time Doc handed the tray to Chris through the crack in the door he saw her face more haggard, with the life and serenity of it vanished, and he would stamp down to the Melodian for whisky. He heard talk of how Ed Briedehoff, left utterly alone by Sheriff Nance, had his north Basin ranchers out riding the country for Ben Mellish, and more than once Doc was tempted to drop a hint as to Ben's whereabouts. Only the thought of Chris kept him from it.

The third day of it, when Doc took in Chris's breakfast to her, he could not bear the look in her eyes. He elbowed past her into the room and glared belligerently around him. Ben was sitting in the only comfortable chair pulled up against the drawn window curtains. He looked more surly than ever, and even his paleness was beginning to fade against the glow of his animal health.

Doc said passionately to Chris, "When are you going to kick him out?"

Chris only shook her head, while Ben laughed unpleasantly.

"When can I walk again, Doc?" he asked.

"The sooner the better," Doc said bluntly.

"I tried to walk today and couldn't," Ben said angrily. "What's the matter with me? I'm weak."

"The trouble with you," Doc said savagely, "is that you are afraid, Ben. You were never hurt bad in the first place —only scared. And damn well you might be. The first time one of these north Basin ranchers lays eyes on you, I'll be called to attend you again—and this time in the capacity of coroner."

"Uncle Doc," Chris said gently. Doc sighed and looked at her. She was paler than Ben, and there was a look in her lifeless face that gave him more than a clue to what she had been going through. It was a look of patient, harried, frantic waiting, and Doc knew surely that if Ben Mellish did not leave soon, she would break. If Doc had known the whole truth he might have been angrier than he was, for Ben Mellish, as soon as he found that his only hurt was a loss of blood, had sunk into a brooding, sullen bullying that Chris was finding unbearable.

The waiting on him and attending him she did not mind, for she was used to that; but his savage impatience, his sneers, his brutal relish of what he had done and of what he was going to do sickened her. There was no relief from it, for she could not leave the house. Since she had last known him in their home, he had changed from a headstrong, rough man into a homicidal monomaniac. He related the story of all his night raids, and laughed when she asked him to stop. And all through his talk and thoughts ran the thread of revenge. He was not down yet. He had money banked, and money would buy help. In the end he would have this Basin at whatever cost. At times Chris pitied him, at others hated and feared him, and he was slowly breaking her. The only thing holding her to him was the thought that they were the children of one mother, and that she must help him. But sometimes as she lay awake on the cot and watched him staring at the lamp, his face secret and crafty and brutal, she wondered if she was sane.

On the fifth day, Pete and Colonel Knight rode into Ten Troughs. Pete had heard no word of the progress of the Basin war, but he did not believe Ben Mellish had been wasting his time.

When Colonel Knight, who remembered Pete's account of the trouble, saw this cattle town lazing in the hot sunshine of late spring, peaceful and serene and busy, he observed, "It seems quiet enough."

"It is," Pete answered. "Too quiet."

Colonel Knight glanced at his friend, puzzled, but Pete's hard and angular face was unresponsive, more sober than he had ever seen it. At daylight they had left the reservation together, and Colonel Knight had ridden the entire day with a mind free of worry. After burying Waranrode they returned to the agency, and found Lassiter's cook and Alphonse Schumacher already under guard. Brief questioning verified everything that Pete had told Colonel Knight, and he, with the memory of Waranrode's suicide fresh in mind, and the possibility that he had blindly been the cause of it, felt an unspeakable burden lifted from his shoulders. All that remained was to get Trueblood's evidence, and to threaten Ben Mellish into a confession. But if Pete felt relieved there was no sign of it on his face, and Colonel Knight wondered in silence.

Pete entered the business section with caution for he remembered his parting with Ben Mellish. When they met again anything might happen. But no one gave them more than a passing glance, and that only because of the strange sight of army blue. Pete rode flat and tense in the saddle, his eyes restless and dark against his browned face.

Reining up, Pete looked toward the Melodian. There were no Anchor horses at the tie rail, no Anchor riders loafing on the sidewalk. Immediately his gaze swiveled to the Legal Tender. In front of it he could see Ed Briedehoff's pony standing hipshot in the sun.

Pete murmured, "You wanted cigars, Colonel. Go get them and meet me here."

He swung off his horse and walked the few yards to the Legal Tender. Two strangers to Pete were drinking at the bar. A desultory poker game was in progress at the window table. He knew none of the players. About to go out, he spied a form on the lone pool table at the rear; and he walked back. It was Ed Briedehoff, unshaven, haggard, deep in sleep.

Pete shook him hard before he wakened.

"What's happened?" Pete wanted to know.

Ed sat up and shook his head, and then looked at Pete, and the light of a deep friendliness lighted his eyes. "I knew you'd be back. You're late, though."

"Late?"

"The fuss is over. Ben Mellish is whipped. He ain't dead yet, but every rider of his is dead or gone. Ben's hidin' out and he's hurt. The Anchor is empty." Paused, he regarded Pete's clean-shaven face, his washed clothes, feeling his restlessness and his strength, and he said, "All we needed was that rawhidin' you gave Steve. It worked."

Pete's slow grin was spare, inquiring.

"You were wrong about Steve. He's fought with us, got shot with us, ate with—"

"Shot?" Pete cut in.

Ed nodded. "In the back. But he ain't hurt bad. That was the last thing Ben Mellish done before he left. Steve's over at Doc Benbow's, and Doc says—"

But Pete had already left. In his haste to get to Doc

Benbow's he forgot about meeting Colonel Knight. He didn't knock on Doc's office door, and he found it deserted. Going into the kitchen, he saw Mrs. Carew and nodded to her and then turned into the bedroom.

Steve lay in bed, his tow hair rumpled and untidy. He had been sleeping and Pete wondered if that pallor was not close to death. Then Steve opened his eyes and for a moment they only stared at each other.

Then Pete grinned broadly. "You piebald road-runner," he murmured. "So they couldn't kill you?"

He took Steve's hand and wrung it, and Steve grinned with delight.

"It's done, Steve," Pete said then. "Waranrode is dead— by his own hand." And Steve listened with grave and rapt attention while Pete told him, and at the end of it Steve looked thoughtfully at the ceiling.

"What about you?" Pete asked. Steve related that grim history of hard-ridden days and nights, and Pete saw that he did not like to speak of it. He was answering Pete's few questions when he said suddenly, "How are we going to break it to her?"

"Who?"

"Sylvia." Then, by way of cryptic explanation, he said, "She's been my nurse through this."

Pete looked at him curiously, searchingly, and a slow flush began to spread over Steve's homely face, but he did not smile.

"I can't help it, Pete. For days now I've been thinking what you're thinking now. You see—" He paused, to see if Pete understood.

"A man couldn't help loving her," Pete murmured. "Is that what you're trying to tell me?"

Steve nodded. "Only it won't work, son. I—I helped to kill her father," he said bitterly, searching Pete's face for a denial.

"Let me answer that. I have known her a long time, Steve. She would rather have him dead if she knew it."

"But why did I have to do it?" Steve said savagely.

"You didn't. I did."

Steve raised his eyes to Pete. "But I helped."

"If you had known Sylvia before this happened, would you have acted any other way?"

Steve sighed. "Maybe I would. But I would have been ashamed of it all my life if I hadn't fought him."

"Don't you think she'll see that?"

Steve did not answer. Pete stepped to the window and looked out. He was waiting for something inside him to resent Steve's love for Sylvia, to be jealous. But there was nothing—and he knew that he had been right that night in the Exchange House.

He heard Steve murmur, "You're a comfort, Pete. Maybe you're right. But I'll tell her some day—before I ask her to marry me."

"Not now."

"No."

All of that part of him that had to do with Sylvia was dead now, Pete knew, and he felt a relief mingled with gladness. And as he felt this die, he felt the other thing within him that he had fought down and smothered these weeks. He said, "Where is Chris?"

Steve turned his head and looked at him. "So that's the way it is?"

Pete said simply, persistently, "Where is she?"

"The shack down the alley back of this place. She's sick, Sylvia says," and he added, "but not very. There's no one with her."

They heard the outer door close and Steve looked swiftly at Pete. "It's Sylvia."

"Let me tell her," Pete said.

In a moment Sylvia entered the room, and at sight of Pete she stopped, and there was a studied moderation in her greeting. "Hallo, Pete."

Pete rose and came over to her and said, "I don't know how to tell this to you, Sylvia, except in the only truthful way."

She caught some of his gravity. "What?"

"Your father is gone. Dead."

She stood utterly still, looking at him, at his eyes.

"It was a hunting accident," Pete said gently. "He was killed instantly."

A moan caught in Sylvia's throat, and she bowed her head. Pete stood aside as she walked over to Steve and kneeled by his bed and put her arms on the spread. Her hand sought Steve's as she began to cry brokenly.

Steve caught Pete's eye and motioned him out, and Pete left. Perhaps this was the way it was meant to be, he thought, as he tramped through Doc's office. Sylvia had turned to Steve in her grief, not to him.

Outside dusk had begun to fall, and Pete looked up the alley. He saw the shack, with its single curtain pulled. Deep within him he acknowledged simply that this was the hour, the minute that he had been waiting for, fighting for; and he turned up the alley, his long stride hurrying a little.

At the shack door he knocked gently, and then opened the door and stepped in.

In one swift glance he saw Ben Mellish sitting in a chair, the fading light of day from the window full upon him. And by him, Christina stood, utterly motionless, her hand half-raised to her parted lips.

In one brief instant Pete knew that he was facing what he had feared most, and what he had tried and sworn to avoid.

A gun was in Ben Melish's hand. With his free arm Ben brushed Christina back, and she cried, "Pete! Pete!"

The gun tilted up, and still Pete could not move, could not unlock his muscles. And then the gun went off, far louder than Ben's snarl. Pete felt the vicious blow on his shoulder and it threw him back and sideways against the door, and the second shot blasted out, missing him.

Chris had turned, and Pete saw her sweep up the lamp from the table, sobbing. And that gesture freed him, striking a spark that ignited movement.

He leaped to one side, at the same time swinging his hand down to the gun in his waistband and it came up in his fist, shoulder-high. He shot five times, so quickly his third shot played its counterpoint against Ben's third shot

—only Ben's stabbed the floor at his feet.

Slowly, an expression of pure amazement on his face, Ben put both hands on the arm of his chair and struggled to heave himself up. Then he sank back and his head fell onto his chest and his gun clattered to the floor.

Pete raised bleak eyes to Chris, and met her horror-stricken gaze for one long moment. Then she folded silently to the floor, the lamp chimney tinkling into splinters.

Slowly Pete moved over to her and kneeled by her. He knew his bullets had not touched her, but she was as dead to him as if they had.

Picking her up he laid her gently on the bed and then left the house. Doc Benbow was running down the alley toward the sound of the shots. At sight of Pete he stopped, and a look of understanding came into his ruddy face.

"Take care of her, Doc," Pete said quietly. "So help me, I've killed him," and he walked beyond Doc and into the street. When he came to the hotel he asked for a room and went up.

He sat on his bed and let the dusk stir into night around him. All the shapes and shadows of these bitter weeks moved in his thoughts, and beyond them and before them he saw the image of Chris as she had looked at him over the body of her dead brother—the brother he had killed. It made no difference to him that he had not sought the fight, nor acted first. It was enough that he had killed him, and in doing so had killed that only other thing he cared for.

As the night grew thick and dark about him, these memories became unbearable, and he rose and walked to the window which overlooked the shadowed street. His shoulder hurt, irritated him.

He must ride on, ride out of here.

He did not at first hear the knock. When he did, he did not answer it. Only when the door opened he turned, a curse on his lips.

There was the figure of a woman in the door. She said, "Pete." It was Chris.

Wordlessly he moved over to the table and struck a

match and lighted the lamp, and then, holding himself taut and careful, he looked up at her.

She moved over to him, her face sad and beautiful and desirable, so that it was a physical hurt for him to look at her.

"I couldn't let you go thinking I hated you," she said.

Pete said bleakly, "Why did I have to be the one who did it?"

"You did it to live."

Despair welled up in him. "Yes. Why do I have to live?" he said harshly. "I never wondered that till now. A moment before I stepped through your door I had pride and love for a woman. I left it a murderer."

"Not a murderer, Pete, for Ben had to die that way. You told me long ago that he would, and that it might be you. And still I stayed on, and helped him and hid him."

"Because you thought you could help him, change him."

Chris only shook her head. "Not entirely. It was because you were here, Pete—and when you weren't near I didn't care if I lived. I didn't live."

For one brief instant Pete stood motionless, and then he took a step toward her, and she was in his arms, and he could not speak.

"Darling, I've waited," she murmured. "Can't we forget it all?"

Pete said huskily, "Before this hour, nothing has ever happened. Remember that, because we can't look back. Will you ever want to?"

"Not if you are with me, Pete."

And Pete knew that it was all behind them, vanished; but he could not say it for kissing her.